In Search of Love

Desperate to be loved, Judith is determined to find her real mother – and her own identity.

At Stone Pillars, she finds a strange and fragile happiness. At first only Daniel guesses her secret. But when the truth comes out, all Judith's hopes seem to be destroyed.

Will she never find the love she is looking for?

In Search of Love

AUDREY CONSTANT

A LION PAPERBACK
Tring · Belleville · Sydney

Copyright © 1985 Audrey Constant

Published by
Lion Publishing plc
Icknield Way, Tring, Herts, England
ISBN 0 85648 903 4
Lion Publishing Corporation
10885 Textile Road, Belleville, Michigan 48111, USA
ISBN 0 85648 903 4
Albatross Books Pty Ltd
PO Box 320, Sutherland, NSW 2232, Australia
ISBN 0 86760 624 X

First edition 1985

All rights reserved

British Library Cataloguing in Publication Data

Constant, Audrey
  In search of love.—(A Lion love story)
  I. Title
  823'.914 J   PZ7
  ISBN 0-85648-903-4

Printed and bound in Great Britain by
Cox & Wyman Ltd, Reading

Chapter One

I watched the bus disappear round the corner. Then, with a feeling of apprehension, I turned up the collar of my duffle jacket and, plunging my hands into the pockets, I set off down the lane. It was January and winter held the forest in its grip. Fallen leaves were crisp under my feet and thin layers of ice covered the puddles at the side of the road. There wasn't a house in sight but I could smell bonfires, so there must be a garden somewhere near.

After about ten minutes I passed a house with a car parked in the drive, frost covering the windows, but I still had further to go. I had been told it was a mile off the main road, and that a car would be sent to meet me, but I had refused the offer. I wanted to walk. It gave me time to think of what I was going to say. There could be no room for mistakes at this interview.

The lane narrowed and along the grass verges a couple of ponies grazed, their manes tangled and touched with white, their breath steaming on the cold air. They moved off into the forest as I came closer. A cold wind brushed my face, catching at my long dark hair and lifting it back over my shoulders.

Now it came to it, I felt desperately nervous. Supposing I didn't get the job? My qualifications amounted to practically nothing − a job in a department store back home and some waitressing in the village recently. My age must be against me too. The advertisement had said a woman was needed. Were you a woman at nineteen? There would certainly be searching questions and some of them I would somehow have to avoid.

The determination which had brought me this far seemed to be slipping away. I tried to recapture the certainty that what I was doing was right. I had felt that all along and now I had become too involved to turn back. In any case, where would I go? They wouldn't want me back home. I had brought enough trouble to my parents already. Besides, I thought, as I walked on, my head bent against the wind, if I don't go ahead with this now, I shall regret it for the rest of my life.

I glanced at my watch. It was already three o'clock and I had walked about a mile without passing a soul. I must soon come to the stone pillars which I had been told marked the driveway to the house.

I came upon them suddenly, as I rounded a corner. The long driveway was overshadowed by trees. I hated firs, at least these dense ones standing so close together that they kept out the light. But after about fifty yards the drive opened into a garden with a wide lawn, surrounded by flower beds filled with trees and shrubs. The earth had been newly dug.

I paused for a moment in the shadow of the trees and looked at the house. I had imagined a cottage where a woman perhaps lived alone, but this house was large enough for a family. It stood, stark and unadorned, built of stone with white doors and windows. Then, my feet crunching the gravel, I walked quickly up to the front door and rang the bell.

With thudding heart, I listened for footsteps and was about to ring again when the door slowly opened and I looked down at a woman in a wheelchair. She must have been in her early forties and although there were lines on her forehead, she was still attractive.

'Could I see Mrs Carey?' I said. 'I have an appointment. My name is Judith Harman.'

'I am Mrs Carey. Come in. I hope you had no difficulty

in finding us. It's a long walk from the bus.' She turned her chair with ease and I followed her through the hall into a large comfortable sitting room.

It was in sharp contrast to the room I had so often imagined and it imprinted itself on my mind in detail, the pale green walls and floral patterned chairs. The french windows overlooked the lawn and the trees beyond. A peaceful room, I thought. A log fire burned in the open grate and at the other end a grand piano took up most of the space.

My attention returned to Mrs Carey as I waited for her to question me.

'Sit down, Judith,' she said, pointing to one of the large comfortable-looking armchairs. I would have felt at a disadvantage on one of those, so I took a small upright chair and clasped my hands in my lap.

She manoeuvred her chair on the other side of the hearth and studied me quietly for a moment. I felt uncomfortable under her scrutiny, though her eyes were kindly and uncritical.

'You didn't expect to see an invalid, did you?' she said presently. 'Perhaps I should have warned you but I dislike talking about it over the phone.'

The advertisement had asked for a companion, not a nurse. I hated illness and hospitals. 'I haven't had any nursing experience,' I said.

She smiled then. The lines disappeared and she looked quite young. 'I can look after myself perfectly well, except for a little help here and there. But I do need someone to do light duties in the house, help me with things I can't manage alone, that sort of thing. I need someone for a month or so until we can make more long term arrangements. You understand that, don't you? It's not a permanent situation.' She had a soft voice with a slight accent which I couldn't place.

7

'Yes. I understand that,' I said. I thought I could manage the things she mentioned. I watched her as I waited for the next question. She looked gentle and rather vulnerable, but there was no sense of recognition, no familiarity about her. Slowly I relaxed, my apprehension receding. I thought I could even like her.

'Before we talk, what about a cup of tea?' She leaned across and pressed a bell near the fireplace. A moment later, the door opened and an elderly woman wheeled in a trolley with tea and cakes. She was a large, cheery individual with grey hair pulled back in a bun.

'Mrs Bill's been with us many years, haven't you, Mrs Bill?'

'More than I'd care to count,' said the woman, placing the trolley within reach of her employer. 'There now, can you manage?'

'Well, Judith,' said Mrs Carey when the woman had gone. 'Tell me why you applied for a job like this?'

'I needed a job and I saw the advertisement in a shop window in Gatehurst,' I said.

'Do you live in Gatehurst?'

'No. My home's in Derby, but I wanted to come south.'

'How long have you been down here then?'

'About six weeks.'

'Staying with friends?'

'Yes.' My landlady could count as a friend. 'I'm working in a café.'

'So you don't think you'll be lonely here?'

'No. I like the country.'

'Have you had any other jobs?'

'Yes. I worked for a department store in Derby for eighteen months.'

'And how old are you?'

'Nineteen.'

'Quite young. I really had someone older in mind. Most young people prefer town life. My son comes home for the school holidays and my daughter from time to time. She used to live at home but she's in London now studying music. My husband is away a lot on business, but is often home at week-ends. That's why I need someone to sleep in at night. He insists that I should not be alone. You understand that you'll be living in?'

'Yes, that's all right.'

'Mrs Bill stays whenever we want her, but it's getting a bit too much for her on her own, though we do have someone else to help out occasionally. As you can imagine your hours will be rather irregular but I think you'll find you have plenty of time off. Will you be happy with these rather vague arrangements?'

'Oh yes.'

'You said your parents live in Derby? I expect we can arrange for you to visit them at least once while you're here.'

'Oh no. I wouldn't need to do that,' I said. 'They won't mind if they don't see me for a month or two.'

'Anyway, we'll see,' she said. 'Now, you'll want to know about payment.' She outlined what she said she had discussed with her husband. It seemed generous enough to me but I wasn't really worried about the wages.

'That's fine,' I said.

'Have you got any reference or testimonial you could let me see? Perhaps from your last job?'

'This is from the department store I worked for,' I said, opening my bag and drawing out a letter which I passed to her. It was quite a good reference.

She read it and appeared satisfied. 'Thank you,' she said, handing it back to me. 'It looks perfectly all right. When would you be able to begin?'

'At the moment, I'm working as a part-time waitress in a café in Gatehurst,' I said. 'It's on a weekly basis so I can leave at the end of the week and come on Friday.'

'Good. We'll send the car to pick you up. You must

have luggage.' She rang the bell and a moment later Mrs Bill appeared. 'Judith will start with us at the end of the week. Would you show her the house and her room and then Daniel can run her back to the village.'

Mrs Bill turned to me. 'Would you like to come with me then?'

I followed her out of the room and upstairs. It was a large rambling house with high ceilings and long passages. I thought it would take a while to clean and wondered if that would be one of my jobs. We went along a corridor with several doors and she opened the end one. 'Your room,' she said.

I liked the room with its sloping ceilings and pretty curtains. I walked over to the window and looked out onto a cobbled yard and stables. A young man was filling some buckets with water but his back was turned. I could hear him whistling as he worked.

Mrs Bill was not a talkative woman and led the way from one room to another.

'How does Mrs Carey manage the stairs?' I asked.

'They had a lift built in after the accident,' she said. 'There it is at the top of the stairs. Now I'll show you the kitchen. You'll be doing some cooking, I expect. Is that what Mrs Carey said?'

'Yes. I'm not very experienced, but I'd like to try.'

Downstairs she opened the door into the kitchen. 'It's all modern,' she said. 'Easy to work in. Edith comes from the village twice a week and does the cleaning so we're not overworked. She's a good woman, is Mrs Carey. It's a shame something like that should happen to her.'

'How did it happen then?' I asked.

'It was a car accident. Now then, you come along with me to the yard and we'll see if Daniel can run you to the village. He's my grandson.'

She opened the back door and led the way across the yard towards the young man I had seen from the window.

He was tall and broadly built, wearing jeans and a grey sweater. He had thick dark hair and a strong profile. He looked a bit older than me.

'Mrs Carey wants you to take this young lady to the village,' Mrs Bill said to him.

He finished filling the bucket before he stood upright and looked briefly at us.

'I've got to bring the horses in,' he said, picking up the bucket.

'That can wait. It won't take half an hour there and back.'

'Half an hour's too long.' He looked at me coolly with piercing blue eyes. 'If she'll wait while I let the horses in, I'll take her,' he said to Mrs Bill, ignoring me completely.

'Is that all right, then?' Mrs Bill asked me. 'Come and wait in the kitchen if you like. I've got to get back there. I've something in the oven.'

'I'll wait here,' I said. There were some bales of hay in the corner of the yard and I walked over and sat on one of them.

Daniel finished filling the buckets and carried them into the looseboxes. Then he began to measure out the food. He didn't even glance in my direction as he worked.

'How many horses have you got?' I asked, more to make conversation than because I was interested.

'A couple and a pony that pulls the trap.'

'Do you work here all the time then?'

'Looks like it,' he said, fastening back the doors of the looseboxes. 'I do the garden too. You'd better move or the chestnut won't go in. She's nervous.'

I moved to the other side of the yard and watched him as he went down the lane towards a field where the horses stood by the gate. I could hear him talking to them and then when he opened the gate they came down the lane, into the yard and each horse went into its own box. He was right about the chestnut, though. She stopped when she saw me. Daniel came up behind her and gave her a slap on the side. Ears pricked and snorting gently, she stepped daintily into her box. He closed the door. Then he turned to me.

'Come on, then. I'll take you now.'

I didn't mind waiting, but I disliked being treated as though I was a nuisance. I hadn't asked to be taken back.

'There's no need if you're busy,' I said. 'I can catch a bus.'

He seemed to relent. 'No. I've been asked to, haven't I? Sorry I kept you waiting, but I had to get the animals in. It's likely to rain again.'

I waited while he disappeared into the garage and backed out a green car. He leaned across and opened the passenger door and I got in beside him. He drove down the drive quietly whistling to himself and keeping well into the side when we reached the narrow road.

'Come for the job?' he asked suddenly.

'Yes. How did you know?'

'They've been coming all the week.'

'Who?'

'The people who come for the job. They don't seem to suit Mrs Carey and I can't say I blame her. They're a strange bunch.'

'Thanks.'

'I didn't mean you. Are you going to take it?'

'Mrs Carey offered it to me.'

'Then you could do worse. She's all right. It's a shame about the accident.'

'When did it happen?' I hoped he would be more forthcoming than Mrs Bill.

'Two years ago. They were coming home from a party. Mr Carey was driving.'

'Was it his fault then?'

'That's what they said.'

I wanted to learn as much as I could while he was willing

12

to talk.

'Does he come home often?'

'He's away a lot on business. Europe and America. He comes when he can. There's a son and daughter too. The girl doesn't do as much as she could for her mother, I'd say, but the boy's OK.'

'How old are they?'

'Sophie's eighteen and the boy a bit younger.'

'Have they lived here long?' I asked presently.

He shrugged. 'The children were born here, I think.'

We were on the outskirts of the village now. 'It's the second turning on the right,' I said. 'You can drop me at the end of that road.'

'OK.' Presently he drew into the kerb and I got out. 'Thanks,' I said as he drove off.

As I walked down to the bungalow where I had rented a room for the last six weeks, I thought that in the end it had all been easy.

I'd got the job. Now it was up to me. Perhaps if I worked well they would not need anyone else and I could stay on. On the other hand, once I'd satisfied my curiosity, it might be better to leave.

But the feeling of bitterness was strong. I had to know what sort of woman would part with her baby. What possible reason could any woman have for doing such a thing? For that was what my mother had done.

Chapter Two

If I had been happy I might never have wanted to find my real mother. Some adopted children get on all right with their parents and don't think too much about their beginnings. But it wasn't like that for me.

I suppose I had a strong streak of independence and because my parents were overstrict there were constant arguments. There were many times when I ran up to my room in floods of tears and slammed the door. Mum tried to understand and keep the peace but in the end she was influenced by Dad and it was always me who was in the wrong.

To be honest I don't think they meant to be unkind. It was just that they didn't understand young people. It was difficult to imagine that they had ever been young themselves. They just behaved old.

As I grew up rows became more frequent. My friend, Annie, was allowed much more freedom than I was. Her parents didn't check on everything she did, but I had to tell mine where I was going and who with. I rebelled and told them the truth even when I knew they would object. I could have lied for the sake of peace, but I was not going to resort to that. The atmosphere became so tense that I spent as little time as possible at home.

Things might have improved. But there was one thing I would never forgive. My parents had always made out I was their own child. They did not tell me I was adopted. And I would not have known if it had not been for my aunt. My parents went away for a few days and she came to look after me. I was fourteen at the time. I suppose I was a difficult kid, because I didn't get on well with her either.

One day I had been to Annie's house and was late home. There was a row. My aunt was so angry her face was white and pinched. Suddenly she blurted out that I was nothing but a worry to my parents and my own mother would not have done so much for me as they had.

The full meaning of what she said did not immediately strike me. But later I really began to wonder. Had she said it to upset me or was it really true?

I said nothing more to her about it and did not even ask my parents when they came home. Then one evening when we were all together in the sitting room after tea, I said, 'Is it true that I'm adopted?'

There was a shocked silence while Dad put down his paper. I saw Mum glance at him before she said, 'Whatever gave you that idea?'

'Aunt Mary.'

'You mean she told you you were adopted?' She sounded incredulous, but whether it was because she couldn't believe her sister would tell or whether she was trying to pretend it was not true, I could not tell.

'She said something that made me think I was. Please will you tell me? I have a right to know.'

Dad took over then. 'Perhaps you have. We never told you because we've always looked on you as our own child and there was no reason for you to think otherwise. But it is, in fact, true.'

I felt blind rage fill my whole being, blotting out reason. It exploded in a torrent of words.

'How could you?' I threw at them, springing to my feet. 'How could you be so dishonest? Why did you never tell me? Everyone has a right to know who their parents are. It was a dreadful, deceitful thing to do.'

'Sit down, Judith.' Mum's face crumpled. 'Give us a

chance to explain. We thought it was best like this.'

'Best for who?' I was shouting. 'Were you afraid of the neighbours knowing? Did you think it would make me like you less? What reason was good enough to keep the truth from me?'

'Sit down, Judith,' Dad said sharply, 'and I'll tell you.' I obeyed him and slowly sank onto the couch. 'We wanted a child. We couldn't have one ourselves, so we chose to adopt you. We brought you up with all the loving care we would have given to our own. We intended to tell you one day, but the time never seemed right and now you've reached an age when you might have understood, you haven't exactly been in the right frame of mind to accept it.'

Mum was crying. 'We hoped you would never find out,' she said, 'at least not before we told you ourselves. I think we would have told you anyway soon. I had no idea you would get so upset by it. What difference does it make anyway?'

'What difference?' I exclaimed. 'All the difference in the world. Who is my mother then? Who do I belong to?'

'Calm down,' said my father. 'You belong to us. When we adopted you, you became legally ours and that's an end to it. It was done through an adoption agency in Southampton, miles away from here. Your natural mother has nothing more to do with you. That was the agreement.'

'But why did she want to get rid of me? Where is she now?' Questions flooded my mind and I couldn't believe that they were unable to answer them.

'It was a long time ago,' said Mum, 'and it makes no difference. In every way you belong to us and we shall continue to do our best for you.'

'It won't ever be the same again,' I said dramatically. 'I can't ever trust you again.' And I stormed out of the room.

It wasn't mentioned again after that. There was nothing further to say. For days we treated each other like strangers and it was on my mind all the time. I talked to Annie about it and she helped me to accept it. In fact, as time went on, I was almost glad. I had so often felt guilty at my inability to get on well at home. Surely everyone should love their parents, at least some of the time, even if they did quarrel with them. I was different. I never really felt I belonged to them or they to me. Now I knew why.

Gradually, things seemed to improve. I told myself that I had much to be grateful for. After all, they had taken me on and given me a home when my own mother disowned me. I tried hard to do better by them, but it wasn't easy. The ties between us had never been close and now, when understanding, love and trust were needed to heal the breach, there was little there. When I went to Annie's house, I noticed with longing the easy, loving relationship between her and her sister and their mother. There were disagreements, of course, but they understood each other. They listened to each other's points of view. There was give and take. I thought at the time that it must always be like that between natural parents and their children. It took me some time to realize that this was not always so.

Annie said it depended on the family. 'I'm lucky, Judith. Our family gets on together, but I don't think it has anything to do with whether you're adopted or not. It's just unfortunate you and your parents are so different. They are terribly strict. I don't think I could stand it, either.'

Then one day she said casually, 'Did you know that adopted children can get help to find their natural mothers?'

'How do you know?'

'I read it in a magazine. It's a new law. I cut it out for you.' She delved into her bag and brought out a crumpled paper cutting and handed it to me. 'You can't do anything

17

about it till you're eighteen,' she said.

It was the summer term. At the end of it I would be leaving school. I already had a job lined up for myself in a department store on a training scheme. I wanted to be independent as soon as possible, and I intended to hand over some of the money to Mum for my keep. But a resolution was slowly forming in my mind and gathering strength. One day I was going to find my mother. But first I would have to earn more money before I could set out on my search.

When I started work, I thought that my parents would recognize my independence and my status. After all, I was no longer a schoolgirl. But I could not even go out for an evening without being closely questioned.

The situation was becoming intolerable. I thought of finding somewhere else to live but it cost too much and besides I had to save every penny if I was ever to make a break and go south in search of a job.

On my eighteenth birthday I went to the Social Services Department. As I sat down to wait, I wondered about my future and my real identity. After ten minutes a young woman called me into her office. I sat down opposite her and waited. She sorted out some papers. Then she looked up at me and smiled. 'How can I help you?' she asked.

I had brought the newspaper cutting with me and gave it to her to read. When she had finished she handed it back. 'So you want to find somebody then?' she asked.

'I want to find my mother.'

She studied me for a moment and then asked if I knew anything about my family history. Had my adoptive parents ever said anything? Did they know that I wanted to find out about my birth?

'No. I haven't told them I want to find my mother. I didn't know I was adopted till I was fourteen.'

She was sympathetic. 'That must have been a shock to

you. Do you think they have any information which would help us in our search?'

I shook my head. 'I don't want to ask them. They just said it was done through an adoption agency in Southampton.'

'That will be some help,' she said. 'Now, the first thing to do is fill in a form.' I waited while she got out some papers and sorted them and then she helped me to fill it in. 'This sort of thing takes time,' she said. 'You'll have to be patient and I must warn you that nothing may come of it. Your mother might not even be alive, or she may have left the country.'

'I know. I'd just like to try, that's all.'

'Very well, then. When I hear anything I'll let you know.'

The weeks dragged. Having taken the first step in my search, I wanted everything to happen quickly. I had already waited patiently for four years and I was as determined as ever to find my mother. It was vitally important to find out about my birth and until I knew, I had nothing on which to build the rest of my life. I might even be a better daughter to my adoptive parents. There was a kind of anger that had taken hold of me and I wanted to be rid of it.

At last I was called for another interview. There were more questions and more explanations needed. Why did I want this information? Would I be satisfied by knowing that my mother was alive or was it my intention to see her?

'Yes, one day, I would like to see her,' I said.

'Can you tell me what you have in mind?' The young social worker was patient and determined to find out all she could from me and I wanted her help so I had to co-operate. It was the system. 'If it could be arranged, would you be satisfied with just one meeting?' she pressed me.

'I suppose so. Does it matter?'

'You understand, don't you, that a meeting might be

upsetting for her? Have you thought about that?'

'Yes. I've thought about it a lot. But I still want to know what she's like and ask her some questions. I wouldn't make a nuisance of myself.'

'You are entitled to the information. The adoption society has been very co-operative. Your mother is alive. Her name is Carey and she lives near a village called Gatehurst. We would, of course, write to her and tell her that you want to get in touch with her. It would only be fair to warn her. You realize she might be married with a family. They might know nothing of your existence.'

'I would embarrass her, you mean?'

She looked at me evenly. 'How would you feel if a young woman suddenly turned up and claimed to be your daughter? Someone you thought you would never see again. How would you explain it to your family who don't know about you?' She said it gently but she had no idea how I felt.

'I would never have my baby adopted in the first place,' I said. 'Never.'

'You don't know the circumstances. She must have believed it was the best thing for you at the time.'

'For herself, perhaps.' I couldn't keep the bitterness from my voice.

Her eyes were sympathetic. 'I do understand how you feel, but we must consider her position too. We want it to be a happy meeting, don't we?'

'Yes,' I said slowly, 'I do. But that's up to her.'

'Judith, if you're angry it's better that you don't see your mother yet. Why not think it over and let us know when you're ready and then we'll write to her and let you know.'

'What if she says no?'

'Then I think we should leave it at that. Nothing useful can be achieved if she doesn't want to see you.'

'No,' I said doubtfully, 'perhaps not. But there's so much I want to know, about my father and why she had me adopted. So many things . . .'

'Of course. I suggest that when you've thought more about it, you come back and see me again.' And that was how it was left.

I didn't go back. It was another three months before I left my job and took a train south. By then I had saved enough to keep myself for a while. I told my parents I was going to stay with a friend and might try and find a job when I was there. We parted on friendly terms and they told me to let them know when I would be back. As I waved them goodbye I wondered if I would ever return.

Chapter Three

I stood looking out of the bungalow window, waiting for Daniel to arrive. Mrs Carey had rung to say that he would fetch me with my luggage.

I had already said goodbye to my landlady. During these last few weeks I had become quite fond of Mrs Baker. She had given me a room when I first arrived in Gatehurst and let me come and go as I pleased, no questions asked. It was she who had told me about the job in the café. And so, as I had something to live on, I had more time to think about how I was going to approach my mother. I had found her name in the telephone directory, the only Carey in the Gatehurst area. I could not, of course, be sure that it was the right one. But, apart from asking the adoption society, there was no way of telling.

Then one day I saw the advertisement in the shop window. That gave me the opportunity I was looking for. I applied for the job and now – I could hardly believe it – I was ready to begin.

The green car drew up outside and, picking up my suitcase, I went out and closed the front door behind me.

'Is this the lot?' asked Daniel, putting it in the boot.

'Yes.' I got into the seat beside him. 'Thanks for picking me up.'

'Just this once,' he said with a hint of a smile in his blue eyes. 'Don't think I'm going to make a habit of fetching and carrying you all over the countryside.'

'No, I won't,' I said seriously. 'I could have caught the bus.'

He ignored that. 'Is that where you live?' he asked as he started the car.

'No, I was only staying there.'

'Oh?' He gave me a quick glance inviting further explanation.

'I've been working in the village and rented a room there.'

'Where do you come from then?'

'Derby. I've only been in this area about six weeks.'

'You don't stay anywhere very long, do you?' he asked. 'I should think you'd soon get fed up in the country.'

'I don't think so. I was in a job in Derby for eighteen months but I don't like living in a town.'

'Eighteen months? What would you say if I told you I'd been in my job for five years?'

'That's a long time and I think you're lucky to have found a job to suit you. I don't think you look that old.'

'Twenty-two,' he said.

We were out of the village now and driving along through open forest when he suddenly said, 'I don't know how long you intend staying with Mrs Carey, but I hope you'll be fair with her. She's had a lot to put up with and she needs someone reliable.'

I felt a prickle of anger. 'What makes you think I'm not? It's nothing to do with you anyway.'

His eyes were on the road. 'No, perhaps not. But if you're going to chop and change to suit yourself, it'll be no use to her. She must be able to depend on you.'

I liked him for defending her, but it made me uneasy. I felt he would be watching me, expecting me to do something wrong. I wondered what it was about me that made him suspicious. Perhaps it was unusual for a girl to take a post like this in the country. I was determined that I would do my best and give no one a chance to complain about my work.

The rest of the journey continued in silence. Presently

23

he swung the car into the drive and pulled up in the back yard. Without a word he took my suitcase out of the boot and carried it to the back door.

'See you then,' he said as he strode off towards the stables. The next moment he was whistling and clattering around in the yard.

Mrs Bill was expecting me. 'So you've come,' she said. 'Now you know where your room is. Go up and unpack and make yourself at home. Mrs Carey is resting. I'll get her down presently.'

I went upstairs and took the things out of my old suitcase. I only had a few clothes with me but I managed to keep them fairly respectable. I was wearing the same black skirt that I wore in the café, and a white blouse. The rest of my things I put away in the wardrobe and drawers and my wash things on the ledge above the basin. My few books I arranged on the table, together with the picture of a bluebell wood I'd always liked. The empty suitcase went on top of the wardrobe. It looked like home already. I felt I was going to be happy here.

When I went down to the kitchen Mrs Bill had a pot of tea ready. We drank it together while she asked me about my family and told me something about the running of the house.

'You'll have your meals with the family,' she said. 'Mrs Carey is often alone and she likes company.'

'I'd rather have them with you,' I said. It would be much more relaxed and what I was used to at home.

'That's what she said. Besides, I'm not here all the time and she wouldn't want you to be lonely. My, it's four o'clock,' she said, looking at the clock on the wall. 'I'll go up and fetch her. She needs a little help when she gets up. Go into the sitting room, will you, and stoke up the fire. I want it warm when she comes down. Then you can come upstairs and I'll show you how the lift works.'

When I went into the sitting room I did not

immediately see the boy sitting in the big armchair, with his back to me. I went over to the fire and was selecting a log from the basket when a voice behind me said, 'Hullo'.

I swung round to see a boy of about sixteen reading a book.

'You're Judith, I suppose. Mother said you were coming.'

'Yes.' I didn't know what to call him, but he went on. 'I'm John. I'm home because I've had appendicitis.'

'Oh, I'm sorry. I hope you're better now.'

'Yes. It's a bore. It would happen in the rugger season. Are you going to live here?'

I smiled at him. I liked his frank way. 'While I'm working here.'

'Good. Mother will be glad. She's been trying to get someone for ages. Since Sophie left really.'

'Who's Sophie?' I asked.

'My sister. She used to help Mother while she was living at home but we had to advertise for someone else when she went to London. They were all pretty useless.'

'I hope I'll be an improvement,' I said. 'I haven't done anything quite like this before, but I can try.'

He was silent for a while, studying me. 'Why did you want to come to a place like this? It must be deadly boring for a girl.'

'I don't think so. I like the country.'

'You're pretty, though. You look more like a town girl.'

I couldn't help laughing. He wasn't bad looking himself. It wouldn't be long, I thought, before he'd be breaking a heart or two. I didn't know what to say so I turned my attention to the fire, poking it to make way for a log.

'Not like that,' he said. 'Here, let me do it.' He pulled a face as he got up. 'It's still sore,' he grumbled.

'How long does it take?'

'Before I can go back to school? About three weeks, I suppose. That doesn't mean a holiday. As soon as I feel up to it or before, I've got to get down to some work. Exams, you know,' he said by way of explanation.

I nodded. I would like to have talked to him longer, but Mrs Bill would wonder what was keeping me. 'I must go,' I said.

'Come back and see to the fire soon, won't you?' he said with a wink.

This boy could be my half-brother, I thought, as I went upstairs. What a strange situation it was.

I heard voices in one of the rooms and knocked at the door. 'Come in, Judith.' I went in. Mrs Bill was about to help Mrs Carey into the wheelchair. I went forward to help. Although she was unable to use her legs, her arms took most of the weight and with our support to steady her, she was soon in the chair and propelling herself across the landing.

'You mustn't think I can't do anything for myself,' she said as she manoeuvred herself into the lift. 'I can do most things with a little help, can't I, Mrs Bill?'

'Of course you can,' said the old lady. 'More than you should, no doubt, but you've got Judith to keep an eye on you now.'

She showed me how to close the doors and push the button from the outside and we went downstairs to meet her.

'Mrs Bill says you've had tea,' she said. 'Come and see me in the sitting room presently, will you?'

I wheeled the trolley in and placed it within reach of Mrs Carey. John was still immersed in his book but looked up and grinned when I came in. When I went in later to get the tea things he'd gone.

'Sit down, Judith,' said Mrs Carey. I obeyed, taking a chair opposite her. 'I hope you're going to be comfortable here. If there's anything you want, you must let us know.'

'Oh, I am, thank you.'

'Mrs Bill will tell you how we do things. It would be best if you have your meals with us. Mrs Bill isn't always here and I'm hoping that she can get home earlier now it's getting wintry.'

'Where does she live?'

'In the cottage down the road. You would have passed it coming here today. Daniel lives with her, ever since his parents died. She and Mr Bill brought him up, until the old man died five years ago. Do you like cooking?'

'I haven't done much. My mother preferred to do that herself, but I'd like to learn.'

'Were you living at home before you came down here?'

'Yes.'

'What brought you down south?'

'I was looking for someone, and then I stayed on.'

Thankfully she didn't pursue it. 'They'll be missing you at home then. When you feel you want to go back to see them, you must let me know and we'll arrange something. I don't want you to feel tied here all the time. We can always get someone to come in and sleep.'

'Does your husband come home often?'

'Usually at week-ends. John's here for a few weeks till he's better and then Sophie comes down quite often. That reminds me — her bike's in the garage. You can use it if you like.'

'Thank you. And the horses? Who rides those?'

'My husband hunts sometimes and John occasionally. Sophie used to ride too, but music took over. What about you? What are your interests? Music, walking?'

'I like both, but I don't play myself.'

'Where did you go to school? Did you enjoy that?'

'Quite. It was a day school near home. I'm not clever. I haven't passed any exams or anything.'

'I expect you're good at other things.'

'I hope so. I really want to do this job well.'

27

I didn't mind talking to Mrs Carey like this. She was friendly and uncritical. She made me feel at ease.

Soon after supper Mrs Bill and I took her up to bed. I knew how to work the lift now and there were various contraptions in the bathroom which enabled her to manage for herself. Mrs Bill had already laid out her nightclothes. And her hairbrush and face creams were beside her bed, and I noticed that there was a Bible there too.

After we had said goodnight and left the room, Mrs Bill said, 'There's a bell beside her bed. She'll ring if she needs anything but she hardly ever does.'

Then Mrs Bill went home. I returned to the sitting room, where John was deep in his book.

'There are plenty of books in the dining room,' he said. 'Help yourself.'

'Thanks. I'll go and choose one and then go up to bed. I'm quite tired.'

'All right, then.' He looked up with a pleasant smile. 'Sleep well. See you in the morning.'

I went up to my room and undressed. Then, turning off the light, I went over to the window. The moon shone on the stable yard and I could hear the horses moving about in their boxes. I wondered what time Daniel finished work and what he did in his free time. Then my thoughts returned to my employer.

What an incredible woman. There she was, confined to a wheelchair for the rest of her life, and yet there was no hint of bitterness in her manner. Everyone seemed to love her. I was sure that if such a thing had happened to me, I would have been bitterly resentful.

I opened the window and drew the curtains. Then I got into bed. It was not long before I was asleep.

Chapter Four

The next morning I was downstairs by seven but Mrs Bill was already in the kitchen.

'What time do you get here?' I asked her.

'Six-thirty. Daniel's always up early with the horses, so I come on over, once I've cleared up at home.'

'You mean you've already had breakfast and cleared up? Whatever time do you get up?'

'We've always been early, ever since my Bill had to get to work in the forest.'

'Mrs. Carey told me he died. I'm sorry.'

'Yes. He's been gone these past five years. The Careys were good to me and let me stay on so I help in the house. Now then, suppose you go and put out the things for breakfast. They don't have anything cooked, just cereal and toast. Then at eight you can go and help Mrs Carey down. She usually manages to dress herself. I put out the things she wants to wear the night before.'

'She manages so well. Will she get better?'

'No. There's no hope of that. She accepts it though. She's got plenty of courage and there's something else besides, I guess it's her faith.'

'Faith?'

'Yes. She draws on some strength outside herself. Something she gets from that Bible of hers.'

The back door opened and Daniel came in with a bucket.

'Any hot water? The mare's got a cough and I reckon a bran mash would put it right.' He nodded at me and then looked at his grandmother.

'Use the tap, or the kettle if it's not hot enough,' said Mrs Bill.

Daniel plugged in the electric kettle. 'Got settled in, then?' he enquired, looking in my direction.

'More or less.'

'Give her time, Daniel. She's only just arrived and she's probably feeling a mite homesick, aren't you, dear?'

'No,' I said, feeling the colour come to my face as Daniel watched me. 'I don't suffer from that.'

Saying I would go and lay the table, I left the kitchen and I could hear Daniel and his grandmother talking. It was sure to be about me.

It was nearly eight o'clock so I went upstairs and knocked on Mrs Carey's door. She was waiting to come down for breakfast.

'Did you sleep well?' was the first thing she said to me.

'Very well, thank you. How are you this morning?'

'I slept well too, but then I usually do. I'm quite ready. I just need a little help to get me into my chair.'

Last night there had been no trouble about moving her, with Mrs Bill there. Now the thought appalled me. Suppose I let her fall? The thought of supporting the weight of that helpless body filled me with unexpected revulsion.

'Just a minute,' I said, gaining time while I struggled to overcome it. 'I'll just hang up your dress.'

'In that wardrobe, dear,' she said.

I opened the door and took out a hanger. I had never seen such an array of dresses. At the other end of the cupboard were shelves of neatly arranged jumpers and undergarments. A lovely scent came from the wardrobe.

What a ghastly thing to happen. As I put the dress away, I could see the scene clearly, not knowing if it really was like that – the dark night, rain, a slippery road, the car swinging out to overtake and the blinding headlights before the final impact as the car swung out of control, pinning her inside. People took risks all the time and usually got away with it. How unfair that sometimes it didn't come off and a few paid for it for the rest of their lives.

'Mrs Bill will tidy the rest later,' the soft voice broke in on my thoughts. 'I just need your support.'

I came over to her and took her weight as she eased herself from the bed. I must have been clumsy after Mrs Bill's capable help, but she told me exactly what she wanted me to do and it wasn't difficult, but I was trembling. I had not foreseen how her disability would affect me and I hoped she would not sense my aversion.

'Good. I can manage now,' she said. 'We'll soon get used to each other.'

'The lift?' I asked.

'I can do that. It was designed for me. I shall go to the bathroom first and I'll be down for breakfast in ten minutes.'

'Yes, Mrs Carey.' I left the room, leaving the door open so that she could get through easily.

John was already down. As we started breakfast, the phone rang and Mrs Bill answered it. 'Mr Carey says he's coming home this evening and will stay over the weekend,' she said, putting the phone down.

Something made me look at John and I was surprised to see the expression on his face. He looked at his mother, his eyes hard. 'I thought he was in Germany,' he said.

'He was. I expect he got home early,' said Mrs Carey gently.

I was in the stable yard when Mr Carey came home. It was late afternoon and Mrs Bill had asked me to get some potatoes from the barn for supper. I was on my way when a black Mercedes drove up and a tall, distinguished-looking man got out. He was about fifty and wore thick-rimmed glasses. He looked briefly at me and then spoke to Daniel, who had just come out of one of the boxes.

'Put the car away, will you, Daniel.'

'Yes, Mr Carey.'

'And you might bring the suitcase from the boot,' he said, walking towards the house with nothing in his hands but a briefcase.

'I'll do that,' said Daniel quietly behind his retreating figure.

'Don't you like him?' I asked, picking out the potatoes and filling the box.

'What makes you think that?' he asked. 'You're right anyway. I don't.'

'Why?'

'Always wrapped up in his work and doesn't give her as much time as he should, to my mind. *You* might like him all right though.'

'Nobody seems to much.'

'You shouldn't be influenced by what other people think. Make up your own mind.' After a pause he said, 'As far as I'm concerned, the more he's away, the better I like it.'

'It's because of the accident, isn't it?'

'No, but he's been much worse since then. He's so bad-tempered.'

'It must be awful for him. Every time he sees her, he must be reminded.'

'Then you'd think he'd want to make it up to her somehow.'

'I don't know,' I said slowly. 'It's funny how something like that affects people. It's strange, the sort of things that make people angry or guilty. You'd think she'd be the one to feel bitter, but she isn't. I would have been.'

Daniel leaned on the pitch-fork and looked at me. 'You're a strange girl,' he said. 'I can't make you out.

32

Something's bugging you but I don't know what it is.'

I bent over the potatoes. 'You imagine things,' I said.

'If you've filled that, I'll take them in for you,' he said and picked up the box and carried it into the kitchen.

I put on an apron and started peeling the potatoes, turning over our conversation in my mind. I could hear Mrs Bill talking to Mr Carey in the hall, then she came into the kitchen.

'When he's home does he help Mrs Carey to bed or shall I take her up this evening?' I asked.

'Sometimes he helps her unless he happens to be working. He always brings a lot of work home. It's best to ask her first.'

'Can I have my supper out here with you tonight?'

'I won't be having mine here. I'm preparing a salad and cold meat and perhaps you could serve it. It's best you eat with them.'

I thought I'd better change out of the clothes I'd been wearing all day and went upstairs. I put on a grey skirt and blue jumper I'd knitted myself and went down to the dining room to lay the table. John was there, looking at a book he'd taken from the shelves which lined one wall of the room.

'Do you like reading?' he asked, looking up from his book.

'Yes, but I don't get much time.'

'You should make time,' he said, with one of his nice smiles. 'You can begin here. There are some good books here. You're sure to find something you like.'

'Thanks. Can I lay the table, or does your father want to work here?'

'No, it's all right. He's in the sitting room boring Mother with his business problems. That's all he thinks about.'

'It's understandable. He seems to work very hard.'

'Too hard. There's more to life than that. I shall never

33

let business interfere with pleasure. I'm not going into business anyway.'

'What are you going to do?'

'I want to be a doctor.'

'Don't you mind looking after sick people? I could never do that.'

He looked at me quizzically.

'Then why on earth did you come to look after Mother?'

I was spared having to answer because, as he said it, something dropped out of the book he held in his hands. I stooped to pick it up and saw it was a photograph of a baby. I looked at it casually. It was old, browned at the edges and partly faded, but it was clearly a pretty baby with a little tuft of hair on the top of its head.

'You?' I asked, handing it to him.

He looked at it closely. 'No. Doesn't look like any I've seen of me. Too pretty. It might be Sophie, I suppose. It must have been here for years.'

'Is it an old book?' I asked.

'Quite old. It's a book of poetry as a matter of fact. I was looking up a quotation. Mother used to read a lot of it.' He put the photo on the dresser.

Mrs Bill had gone home, so I prepared the supper and mashed the potatoes. Then I knocked on the sitting room door and told them it was ready.

'Come and meet my husband, Judith.' Mrs Carey turned to him. 'Harry, I told you about Judith. She came two days ago and already she's been a great help.'

He looked up from the newspaper. 'I hope you're settling in,' he said. 'Do you live locally?'

'No, I told you, dear, she comes from Derby. She's living in at the moment.'

'Until she gets bored stiff like Sophie,' said John. 'Then she'll be off to the bright city lights.' He winked at me.

His mother reprimanded him. 'Of course she won't,' she said. 'Judith is quite free to go anywhere she wants and she'll have plenty of time off for it. We've already discussed that.' We moved into the dining room.

John went over to the dresser and picked up the photograph. 'Look what I found in that book of poetry,' he said, handing it to his mother. 'Is it Sophie?'

She took the photo and looked at it closely. 'No, it isn't Sophie,' she said. 'It's another baby I was very fond of.'

'Who is it?' asked John.

'No one you knew. I lost touch with her a long time ago.'

She looked at me and smiled and for a moment I wondered if she had guessed. Then I dismissed the idea. There was no way she could possibly know. Not unless there was something about me which reminded her.

Chapter Five

'I'm selling the horses,' said Mr Carey at breakfast.

John looked up from a letter he was reading, dismay on his face.

'But why . . . ?'

'They're costing too much and they're not used.'

'We ride them in the holidays,' said John. 'Don't sell Fleet. Please, Dad.'

'She was bought for you, John, but you rarely ride her. Unless she's ridden regularly she'll become impossible to handle.'

'I can't ride her at the moment, but I shall at Easter.'

'Easter perhaps, but you're going to France in the summer and you'll have even less time after that. It costs a fortune to feed those horses through the winter.'

'But what will you do with the land? The horses keep the grass down.'

'Jones next door wants more grazing. He asked me the other day for the option if I sold.'

'Does Sophie know?' asked John.

'Yes. She doesn't want them to go but she agrees she's hardly ever here to ride them.'

'What about Daniel?' Mrs Carey asked. 'Have you spoken to him about it yet?'

'There's nothing to discuss with him. I'll tell him of my decision later.'

I disliked the way he made decisions without discussing them with his family. I was sorry for Daniel too. He loved his horses.

'He'll be upset,' Mrs Carey said. 'He's so fond of them. Besides, there won't be enough for him to do.'

'If you think that, perhaps we'd better find someone part-time. There's still the garden, though, and the trap pony. We'll keep Joey at any rate for the time being.'

'I'd be very sorry to see Joey go,' said his wife. 'But if it's really necessary we'll have to sell the others.'

'It's essential,' Mr Carey said. 'We've got to cut down somewhere. Expenses are rising all the time and the housekeeping bills are enormous – not to mention school fees.' He glanced at John.

'I'm sorry,' said John, tight-lipped. 'I didn't ask to be sent to boarding school.' Abruptly he got up and left the room.

Mr Carey watched him, a frown on his face. 'He's old enough to understand just how much things cost these days and the pressure I'm under to meet all the bills, but he doesn't try to co-operate. The boy's too critical. I don't like to see it.'

His mother defended him. 'He can't do anything to help, though. Not yet. But it won't be long now before he leaves school.'

I gathered up the dirty plates and, glad of an excuse to leave, carried them into the kitchen.

Mr Carey spent the rest of the morning working on the dining room table and that afternoon I saw him talking to Daniel in the yard. Soon afterwards he left for London.

Mrs Bill went home early that evening and John was working in his room. I went into the sitting room with my book. Mrs Carey was there doing some tapestry. She looked pale and tired.

'You mustn't worry too much about this morning, Judith,' she said. 'My husband is working under pressure all the time and when he makes a decision, he doesn't like opposition.'

'Do you mind about the horses?' I asked.

She shrugged. 'It doesn't affect me much, but John's upset. He loves riding.'

'Might he change his mind?'

'My husband? Never.'

'I would be quite happy to work for less, Mrs Carey. Now I'm living in, I don't need much money. Not as much as you're paying me.'

'Bless you. That makes little difference. You're a great help and we need you. Of course you must take it.'

'I don't like to think that I'm adding to the problems.'

'You're not,' she said briskly. 'It's marginal. I just wish the children could be more understanding. They're young, of course, but old enough to know how hard he works and that he wants to do the best he can for them.' She smiled. 'I was probably the same when I was young. It's only when you're older that you look back and understand your parents a little better. We all make mistakes.'

'But surely they must be able to say what they think, even if they disagree with him.'

'There are times to speak and times to keep quiet. I'm afraid they haven't worked out the difference yet.'

'It always seems difficult with families,' I said.

'What about yours, Judith? It sounds as though you have family problems too.'

'I don't get on well with my parents.'

'Tell me about them,' she said, laying aside her work.

'Perhaps it's because I was adopted.'

She showed no surprise. 'But were your parents kind to you?'

'Oh yes, I suppose so. They never actually ill-treated me but I never had much freedom, even when I was sixteen.'

'Sometimes that shows concern for a child. Lack of attention can be worse than too much.'

I shook my head. 'I don't think so. Mum and Dad just

didn't understand how young people feel.'

'Did they know how you felt? Did you ever discuss it with them?'

Oh yes, they knew all right. That's what all those rows were about, but I didn't tell her that. 'I used to try,' I said, 'but Dad got angry and then Mum took his side. I don't think they meant to be unkind. It was just that I wasn't like them. I wasn't their child, you see.'

'Adoption does work sometimes,' she said thoughtfully. 'I'm sorry it didn't for you.'

Should I tell her now, I thought, tell her how in the end I couldn't stand it any more and that I was determined to come and find her? But how was I to begin?

And then the moment passed. I could hear John coming downstairs for supper. I went into the kitchen to prepare it.

The next day was bright and sunny and less cold. Mrs Carey asked me to tell Daniel that she wanted to go into the village that afternoon.

'You come too, Judith. Ask Mrs Bill if there's anything she wants in the village and then we'll drive back through another part of the forest. It's pretty at this time of year when the branches are bare. Tell Daniel we'll start at about two.'

I went out to the stables after breakfast. The horses were still in their boxes. These cold mornings Daniel turned them out later. Even then, they had their coats on. All except Joey, the thick-coated pony that pulled the trap. He was out in all weathers.

Daniel was nowhere to be seen so I went to the loose boxes. I could hear him talking to the chestnut mare. His back was to the door and I don't think he heard me. I stood there for a moment, watching him stroking her. She delighted in his caresses, rubbing her head against him and nuzzling his jacket.

Then, running his hand over her back, he came to the door.

'How long have you been standing there?' he demanded.

'Not long. I've just come out.'

'Another time, don't creep up on me. I don't like being observed.'

'I wasn't observing you,' I protested. 'I came to tell you that Mrs Carey wants to go into the village at two today and have a drive afterwards.'

'OK. I'll get the car out.' He went past me towards the barn and I returned to the kitchen, wondering why his mood had suddenly changed. It must have had something to do with the horses going.

After lunch I stood by while Daniel helped Mrs Carey from the wheelchair into the front seat of the car. He was wonderfully gentle with her, knowing exactly what to do. Once she was in, he tucked a blanket over her knees.

'There now, are you comfortable?' he asked her.

She smiled at him. 'Quite, thank you. What a nuisance I am.'

I got into the back and we set off down the drive. Mrs Carey and Daniel talked about gardening. In Gatehurst we parked the car in the main street and I went into a small supermarket with Mrs Bill's shopping list. When I returned to the car, they were discussing the horses. I thought Mrs Carey had never been interested in them, but it was evident from their conversation that she knew a great deal. She spoke with such authority I realized that she had spent much of her time with horses. I thought sadly that the accident must have put an end to all her enjoyment of riding as well.

When I got in she said, 'Let's go home a different way and show Judith the forest.'

'We'll go through the Ornamental Drive,' said Daniel. 'It's pretty there, though now the weather's getting warmer, people will be coming out in their cars.'

As we came out of the village he turned off into a side road that led through tall trees and over little bridges. Presently we were in open spaces again where groups of ponies grazed together with cattle.

'Are they wild?' I asked.

'No,' said Daniel. 'They all belong to someone. See the distinctive marks they have? Look at that one over there with a brand and that pony with half its tail cut. Twice a year they're rounded up and some of them sold.'

'What about the cattle?'

'They're owned too. People living in the forest have what are called Commoners' Rights. They are old laws that go back hundreds of years. It means they have the right to graze a certain number of ponies or cattle on the forest. In the autumn they turn out their pigs to eat the acorns as well.'

'Don't they get lost? The forest seems so big and I can't see any fences except on the main roads.'

'Oh, they know their area and don't wander far. The plantations, of course, are enclosed, or the deer would be eating all the young trees.' He was so knowledgeable.

He slowed down the car and pulled in to the side of the road where there was a wide view overlooking a marsh. Beyond were great beeches, their bare branches brown against a plantation of firs. The sun was shining, casting shadows on the landscape. We could see for miles and there was no one in sight.

'Look at those colours,' said Mrs Carey. 'What a picture that would make. Maybe, one day, I'll start to paint again.' She sounded wistful.

'You should,' said Daniel firmly.

She smiled, perhaps a little sadly. 'I'm afraid I've left it too long. I don't think I could now.'

We stayed there a while longer and then drove off in the direction of home. On the way back Daniel returned to the subject of the horses.

'When did Mr Carey decide to sell them?' he asked.

'When he came home at the week-end. You're going to miss them, aren't you, Daniel?'

'I will. I was thinking that maybe you wouldn't be wanting me full-time now, seeing that they're going.'

'There's still the garden, Daniel. I hope you won't be thinking of leaving us.'

I leaned forward to catch what he said. I didn't want him to leave either.

'Well, I like the horses, as you know, and they've often asked me to help at the stables in the village, but that wouldn't suit me. I don't mind admitting that I'm sorry to see them go. You've always let me have my way with them and I've grown fond of them, but if that's what Mr Carey wants, we'll have to get used to it, won't we?'

Mrs Carey turned to smile at him. I could see she was as relieved as I was.

Chapter Six

One night I missed the last bus home.

It was my day off and I went into Southampton to do some shopping. It was John's last day at home before returning to school and I thought they might prefer to be on their own.

When Mr Carey was down, I rarely saw John talking to him. Since the argument over the horses, he seemed to keep out of his father's way, going up to his room in the evening. But he was fond of his mother and I often heard them talking and laughing together. The place was lively when John was at home.

I had been at Stone Pillars now for a month and had just received my first wages. I was asked if I wanted it in cash or whether I had a bank account and would like a cheque. I asked for cash. I had no bank account and I needed the money to buy some new clothes.

In Southampton I found my way to the main shopping area and spent some time looking in shop windows and watching the people. It was strange to catch sight of myself in a shop window. I looked out of place in the city. My hair needed cutting and my clothes were old. The next shop was a hairdressers' and, after a quick look at the price-list, I went in. On impulse I asked one of the girls to style my hair. As I felt it falling to the ground I nearly lost my nerve, but afterwards it felt good and I liked my new image. Definitely.

In a department store I bought some underclothes and a blouse and skirt. I had intended to treat myself to lunch but I had little left out of my wage-packet and settled for a coffee and a pastry.

Then I had one more purchase to make. I went into a china shop and bought a small jug in deep blue porcelain. Then, picking up my purchases, I hurried to the railway station. I had no idea how often the buses ran from Gatehurst out into the forest, but I knew they weren't frequent.

When I arrived, the last bus had already left. There could be little demand for buses in the country once people finished work and most country folk had cars anyway. I thought of ringing the house but Mrs Carey would insist on sending Daniel to meet me and I wanted to avoid that. I didn't have enough money for a taxi, so there was nothing for it but to walk.

As I left the village on the main road, the car lights were dazzling. Soon I turned off towards the house and there was very little traffic. There were no houses along this stretch and I seemed to be the only person in the dark forest.

I was glad when I saw the lights of a car coming towards me. At least someone was about. I moved onto the verge as it came closer and then it slowed down. Suddenly I was afraid and ready to run. A voice called out, 'What are you doing, walking along these lanes alone at night?'

I drew a breath of relief. It was Daniel.

'I missed the last bus back.'

'Come on. You'd better get in. I'll run you home.'

Even though I wanted a lift, I didn't want him to think I was scared.

'I'm all right. You're not going that way.'

'I can turn. You're not going to walk back alone at night. Get in.'

Obediently I climbed into the van. It belonged to him and he used it sometimes to come to work. It smelt of country things, a mixture of horses and oil.

He turned and started back along the road.

'If you must be out so late, it would be best to ring the house. If I'm there, I'll come and get you.'

'And if you're not, Mrs Carey will be bothered. It was my own fault that I missed the bus and I don't mind walking. Just the same, thanks for the lift,' I added. 'I hope it hasn't made you late.'

I wondered where he was off to at this time of day, whether he was going to a pub or to meet a girl-friend perhaps. From what I could see in the dark, he looked smarter than usual.

'My time's my own,' he said. 'What have you done to your hair?' He asked this without even looking at me.

'I've had it cut.'

'What on earth for?'

'I wanted a change. How could you see it in the dark anyway?'

'I had to look twice. I didn't think it was you at first. Where have you been?'

'I went to Southampton.'

'To see friends?'

'No. I went shopping.'

'Don't you know any folk around here? It must get a bit lonely at times.'

'No, not with Mrs Carey and Mrs Bill.'

'My gran's concerned about you, you know. She says you're good with Mrs Carey and a help around the place but she can't make you out.'

'What do you mean? There's nothing special about me.'

'She says you never talk about your family. Don't you get on well with them or what?' Mrs Bill never asked me the direct questions that Daniel did. But she had pressed me to take more time off, saying that if I had nowhere better to go, then I could have tea with her. I liked her and intended to do this some time.

'I told you, I came south to look for someone.'

45

'A fellow?'

'No.'

'All right. You want to keep your secret to yourself. I just thought you might like to talk about it. You can trust me to keep quiet if that's what you're worried about.'

'There's a personal reason why I can't tell anyone, Daniel, so please don't press me.'

We had come to the end of the drive. 'Please drop me here. I'm quite all right now.'

He stopped the van and I got out. 'Thanks,' I said as I closed the door. I stood watching as he turned round and drove back towards the village. I wanted to tell him but I couldn't risk it. He had only to mention it to Mrs Bill and then she would tell Mrs Carey. I could never be certain my secret was safe.

The front door was unlocked. Leaving my parcels in the hall, I went into the sitting room where John and his mother were watching television.

'Thank goodness you've returned, Judith,' she said. 'I wondered what had happened to you.'

'I'm sorry. I went to Southampton and missed the last bus home.'

'You didn't walk?'

'Some of the way, then I met Daniel and he brought me back.' John grinned at me and I coloured as I knew he was thinking it was prearranged. 'He happened to be going into Gatehurst,' I said.

'I like your hair,' he said.

'It certainly suits you,' his mother agreed. 'Mrs Bill left something for you in the kitchen. You must be hungry.'

'Thank you.' There was a plate of cold meat and salad on the table, covered with a cloth. I was ravenous and ate it all. Then I washed the dishes and went to find one of my parcels which I took in to Mrs Carey.

'I bought this for you today.'

'How nice of you,' she said as she unwrapped it and held

46

the little jug in her hands. 'Thank you, my dear. It was a lovely thought.' She put it on the table beside her.

'It's only small, but I wanted to say thank you for being nice to me.'

'It is I who must thank you.'

John said he had some packing to do and went up to bed.

'I shall miss him when he goes tomorrow but it's time he went back. He's missed too much school already and he gets bored.'

'It will soon be holiday time,' I said. I had something in mind that I had been thinking about for some time. Now seemed a good time to suggest it.

'The other day you said you used to paint. Did you get rid of your paints?'

She laughed. 'No, I've still got them somewhere. They must be hard and useless now. I might as well throw them away.'

'Let's get them out tomorrow,' I suggested. 'You might enjoy it again.'

'I don't know. I was never much good and I'm quite out of practice.'

'That picture over there is beautiful and you did that.'

'A long time ago,' she said.

'It doesn't matter. I'm sure it's something you never forget. Can I look for them?'

'All right. If you like. I think they're at the top of the cupboard on the landing.'

As I helped her into bed that evening it seemed to me that there was some movement in her hips, but perhaps it was imagination. Everyone had told me that medically it was impossible but surely, if you're determined enough, miracles can happen.

I had long since overcome my feeling of aversion and now I enjoyed doing things for her. I felt her dependence in some way drew us closer together. I wondered if Mrs Bill was right in saying that the inner strength which helped her cope with her life had something to do with her faith. Sometimes, in the morning, I found her reading the copy of the Bible which she kept by her bedside. Whatever it did for my mother, I wished that I could find it too.

Chapter Seven

One day Mrs Bill was off sick. Daniel came in to say that he had got the doctor to her who said it was 'flu. She had to stay in bed and rest for a few days, so I asked if I could borrow Sophie's bike and went round to see her.

Mrs Bill and Daniel lived in an old forester's cottage about a mile down the road which now belonged to the Careys. It was an isolated place with a large garden which Daniel kept. The old lady still managed to cycle to work, except on wet days when Daniel brought her in the van.

I found her sitting up in a chair by the fire.

'You're meant to be in bed,' I scolded her.

'I haven't got time to stay in bed. Only get weaker if I do,' she said.

'Has the doctor given you some medicine?'

'He gave me a piece of paper to take to the chemist, but medicine never did me any good. No. Drink plenty of water and keep warm, that's what I always do, not that I'm often laid up. Managing all right, are you, back at the house?'

'Yes, of course. Mrs Carey says you're not to come back till you're quite well. Look, give me that piece of paper and I'll go and get it for you.'

'No. Daniel said he'd go, but I won't let him. I tell him I'll only throw the stuff away.

'That's silly, Mrs Bill. You'll get better all right without it, but it will take that much longer. Let me have it, please.'

'It's on the table in my room. But I don't want you

bothering. You must have your hands full now, what with Mrs Carey and the cooking and all.'

'My cooking's not too good, but it's surprising what you can turn out if you try, and I've found one of your old cookery books. Can I go to your room?'

'If you want.' I went up the narrow creaky stairs. There was the bathroom and two other doors on the landing both of which were closed. I tried one. Definitely a man's room. Tidy, too. It must be Daniel's. I took a quick look before leaving. Pictures of horses on the wall, a full bookcase and a gun leaning up in the corner. There were some clothes neatly folded over a chair and a masculine smell about the room. The window was slightly open.

I closed the door and went into the other room. Ill though she was, Mrs Bill had made her bed and tidied her room and the window was wide. The room was icy and I went over and closed it. Habits of a life-time die hard, I thought. I found the prescription on the table and came downstairs.

'I'll go into the village this afternoon and get the medicine,' I said. 'I'll bring it round later. Now, is there anything else you'd like?'

'No, dear. It's thoughtful of you.'

'Before I leave, I'd like to see you in bed. Why don't you go up and I'll bring you a hot drink and a bottle.'

'Truth to tell, I do feel a little poorly. I think I'll take your advice.'

I helped her upstairs and then went down to the kitchen. When I got back she was still sitting on the bed.

'Come on, I'll help you,' I said, bending down to take off her shoes. I got her undressed and helped her into her warm flannel nightdress. Then I wrapped a towel round the bottle so it wouldn't be too hot for her. I stayed while she sipped the drink. She was almost asleep when I left.

When I got back, Mr Carey's car was parked in the drive. I really wondered why he bothered to come. He spent hardly any time with his wife and never took her out. If he wanted somewhere to work other than the office, he had a flat in London.

I went off to find Daniel who was planting seeds in the kitchen garden.

'I went to see your Gran,' I said. 'I made her get back into bed.'

'So she got up, did she? I told her she wasn't to.'

'And I've got the prescription. I'll get the medicine this afternoon and take it round to her.'

'You must be very persuasive. She wouldn't let me get it. She said she'd throw the stuff down the drain.'

'I don't think she will. She seemed quite glad to be told what to do.'

'Thanks anyway. How are you getting into the village?'

'Bike. I'll get lunch over with and then go. I see Mr Carey's home?'

'Yes,' he said shortly. 'He wants me to clean the car. I'd better make a start on it. He needs it after lunch, he said.'

'Perhaps he's going to take Mrs Carey for a drive?'

'I doubt it. It's my belief it brings back the memory of that night, though he makes out it's pressure of work.'

When I got back I found Mrs Carey in the kitchen preparing a salad for lunch.

'I can do that,' I said.

'No. I've almost finished. It takes time but I enjoy it.'

'Mrs Bill needs some medicine. Can I go into Gatehurst this afternoon?'

'Yes, of course. Harry's going in, as a matter of fact. You could go with him.'

'Yes, of course. We'll call in at the chemist,' said Mr Carey who had just come into the kitchen to find a beer in the fridge.

'I'd rather cycle,' I said.

'Go with him, dear,' said Mrs Carey. 'He won't be long there, will you, Harry? Then you could drop it off to Mrs

51

Bill on the way back. Tell her I'll get Daniel to drive me round to see her one day.'

'Why don't you come too?' I asked her. 'It would make an outing for you.'

For a moment there was silence. She looked at him, but he was busy opening a can of beer. 'No, dear. It takes too long. Besides I'm expecting a friend this afternoon.'

I felt it was up to him to try and persuade her, but he didn't. It would have been impolite to refuse to go with him, so I agreed and after lunch we set off in the Mercedes. In fact, he was quite pleasant and thanked me for what I was doing for his wife.

'I think it was your idea that she should take up painting again?' he asked.

'Yes, it was and I'm glad she's enjoying it.' She had begun, not very seriously at first, and I think she was only doing it to please me. But recently she had started a painting of daffodils under the trees on the lawn, a scene which she could see through the french windows. Now she spent most mornings working on it. I knew it was good and I saw how utterly absorbed she was.

Mr Carey stopped outside the riding stables before we reached the village, and told me to wait in the car. While I was there a string of rather tired-looking horses came out of the gates with an assortment of riders. Some of them looked very uncomfortable and I could understand how Daniel would dislike working in a place like that.

I wondered what Mr Carey was doing there. Nothing more had been said about the sale of the horses. When he came out he was looking pleased with himself. 'They'll take both the horses,' he said. 'It will save advertising and the bother of people coming to see them.'

'Surely they're too good for riding stables?' I burst out.

His face hardened. 'What do you know about horses, young lady? They'll be well-treated and not overworked. I want to get the matter cleared up.'

He started the car and we drove on into the village where he parked outside the chemist while I went in and got Mrs Bill's medicine.

'Have they shown you where Admiral Nelson built his ships?' he asked as he started the car.

'No. Is it near here then?' I asked.

'Quite close. On the river. We'll run down there now if you like. It's a nice afternoon.'

'But I have to take Mrs Bill her medicine,' I protested. It was the last thing I wanted to do. With the old lady off sick there was plenty to do in the house and I hadn't thought about supper yet. It took me a long time to cook a meal and I could only manage the simplest thing. Sometimes Mrs Carey came out to the kitchen and we managed to produce something. It was fun doing it together.

'Nonsense. A short break will do you good. We'll be back in time for tea.'

He took another road out of the village and the car picked up speed along the straight narrow road. I sat back in the low comfortable seat and wished I hadn't come. His will, usually directed towards other members of his family, had been turned on me and there was nothing I could do about it.

In a matter of about ten minutes we turned onto a roughly-made road which led down to a wide river.

'These days there are plenty of pleasure boats here, but two hundred years ago most of the ships that took part in the Battle of Trafalgar were built here.'

We got out of the car and strolled down to the water's edge. Mr Carey knew a lot about history and, in spite of myself, I was fascinated. Sometime I must get Daniel to drive us down here, I thought.

Back in the car he said, 'My wife says you're a great help to her, Judith. I expect she's told you that I'm looking for a nurse for her. When I'm abroad, which is more frequent

53

these days, I must have an older woman in the house, someone qualified in case something should happen.'

'She told me that the job was a temporary one, but I can manage perfectly well.'

'Just the same, I think it's too much for a young girl to be responsible for an invalid all the time.'

'Mrs Carey isn't an invalid. She's disabled, I know, but she never makes a fuss about it and I like working for her.'

He was silent for a while, then he said, 'You're not a child and I expect you can understand what it's like for me having a handicapped wife. For instance, in my job, I have a lot of entertaining to do. These days I have to do it in town. We can't go away for holidays because she doesn't like leaving the security of her home, though there are places for disabled people. It's understandable, of course, and she's taken it very well, but I must confess it makes it difficult for me.'

I felt anger boiling, and I burst out, 'Whose fault is it she's like that?'

He gave me a quick look and asked in a low voice, 'Whose fault did they tell you it was?'

'Who? No one has told me anything, except it was a car accident. Whose fault was it? Please tell me.'

'I was driving if that's what you mean, but I couldn't avoid the car coming the other way. It was a black night and pouring with rain. We skidded.'

It was useless to continue the conversation. He could so easily make it sound as if he wasn't responsible. But Daniel had said the Court had given the verdict against him. That was conclusive enough.

'Anyway, I didn't bring you here to talk about that,' he went on. 'I wanted to make it a pleasant afternoon's outing and find out if there is something you would like to see, perhaps a play or ballet, when Mrs Bill is back again. I could arrange it and I would like to repay you in some way for your kindness to my wife.'

'No, thank you,' I said stiffly. 'I'm paid for the work anyway and I like working for her.'

He sighed and started up the engine. 'Very well, I just thought you might enjoy it. You've taken a load off my mind by looking after her and I wanted to say thank you in some personal way.'

He sounded so sincere, I almost thought I was wrong in thinking that he was thoroughly selfish.

The forest looked beautiful. The sun was shining and some of the buds opening, but I hated being in the car with him.

'Mrs Bill . . .' I began.

'Yes, we're going back now. You're a thoughtful girl, caring for the old lady, too.' He put his hand lightly on my knee. I sat there frozen. I felt that so easily the situation could get out of control. I had no idea how to handle the advances of a middle-aged man. I'd had no experience. If it had been a young fellow I'd have told him to keep his hands to himself, but, after all, this man was my employer and it might have been nothing more than an attempt at kindness. I felt disgusted though. I sat rigid and tried to move my leg away. He laughed and put his hand back on the wheel.

When we reached the cottage I got out and closed the door. 'Please don't wait. I'll be here some time and I'll enjoy the walk back.'

He shrugged but he didn't argue. With a feeling of relief I saw him disappear down the road and then I went into the cottage.

Chapter Eight

Daniel opened the door. He seemed pleased to see me. 'I came home early today,' he said. 'I wanted to see how the old girl was.'

'How is she?'

'Asleep. I didn't like to wake her.'

'Can I see her?'

He led the way upstairs. Mrs Bill opened her eyes as we came into the room. 'Hullo. I've brought your medicine,' I said.

She struggled into a sitting position and I reached for a jacket and put it round her shoulders. There was a fire downstairs in the kitchen but the bedroom was icy.

'Isn't there some sort of heating she could have?' I asked Daniel.

'There's an old stove in the garage at the house and some oil. I'll get it.'

'She should have something.' I turned to Mrs Bill. 'What do you fancy now? A hot cup of tea?'

'I'd rather have that than medicine,' she said.

'I'll put the kettle on,' said Daniel, as he went downstairs. 'I'll be back in a flash.' He closed the back door and I heard his van start up.

I took her hot water bottle and went down to the kitchen. Everything was spotless though the floor covering was worn and old. I looked into the little sitting room that led off the kitchen. The fire had gone out but it was still fairly warm. I made the tea, filled the hot water bottle and found a spoon for her medicine.

56

Then I went upstairs.

I pulled up a chair by the side of the bed and had a cup of tea, too. Afterwards she took her medicine with nothing more than a disgusted look.

'You'll be as right as rain in a few days, but you've got to keep warm. Daniel's gone to get a stove from the house.'

'I don't often take to my bed,' she said, 'but it's nice to be fussed over.'

'And it does you good. We like to have the chance to do it. You do a lot for us over at the house.'

'You tell Mrs Carey I'll be back just as soon as I can get these old legs to support me.'

'You'll be back no sooner than the doctor says you can,' I warned her firmly.

She chuckled. 'I didn't know you could be such a bully, Judith. You were a meek little thing when you came. Frightened almost, and kind of on the defensive, as though you expected people to find fault with you. Now look at you! Bullying an old woman like me!'

I smiled. Looking back I could see what she meant. It was because I felt at home now. I knew I could cope with my job and this had given me confidence. Because I had grown to love my mother, I thought I could now accept my adoption without bitterness.

I heard the van coming back and the next moment Daniel came in with the oil-stove. He carried it over to a corner of the room and lit it.

'It will probably smell a bit to begin with. Perhaps I'd better open the window,' he said, looking at me.

'Yes, but don't forget to close it before long,' I said, getting up. 'I must go now, but I'll call in some time tomorrow.'

'Have a bite to eat before you go, dear. Daniel, there's a cake in the tin. Light the fire in the sitting room and make her comfortable for a while.'

'I should be getting back,' I said.

57

'Stay for a few minutes,' said Daniel. 'I'll run you back afterwards to save you time.'

'Then I will. Take care of yourself, then, and keep warm,' I said to Mrs Bill.

I followed Daniel downstairs into the sitting room. He brought in some wood and put a match to the fire and soon there was a cheerful blaze.

'Sit down and I'll get some tea.'

'I made some just now for Mrs Bill. It just needs some more hot water.'

I heard him moving about the kitchen, searching in tins, presumably for the cake. Through the lattice windows I could see crocuses and early daffodils. The fruit garden had recently been manured. I wondered how Daniel found time for this garden too. He must spend all his spare time at it. At the bottom of the garden was an old stone building with stable doors.

'Did you keep a horse here once?' I asked as he came in with a tray.

'I had a pony when I was a kid. My father used to work in the forest and I would go with him and ride for miles while he worked. That's when I got to know the forest so well.'

'How old were you when he died?'

'Twelve. He didn't die. He was killed by a falling tree.'

'How awful! Did you see it happen?'

'No. I was at school at the time, but I don't think I shall ever forget when my mother told me. I was upset, of course, but I felt so angry. Why should it happen to him? It took me a long time to get over that. It was Gran who got me to face up to it in the end.'

'What about your mother?'

'She died two years later. I was fond of her, too, but I didn't feel so bad about that. Again it was Gran who helped me through with some straight talking. She was great.'

I walked over to a table on the other side of the room where there were some photographs, and picked one up. I saw a pretty woman with a child with curly hair.

'Is that her?' I asked.

'Yes, with me,' said Daniel, pouring out the tea. 'There's one there of Dad, too.' I picked up the photos and studied them.

'Come and have your tea. It'll be cold.'

'So your gran brought you up by herself?'

'And Grandad, until he died five years ago.'

'But you've always been happy, haven't you?'

He looked at me for a moment. 'Of course. Why shouldn't I be?'

'I think you can stand most things if you've got a good home. If people are kind to you.'

He didn't say anything for a moment. Then, 'You weren't happy, then? Is that what you're saying?'

I shook my head. 'Not very.'

'It's past now, though, isn't it? There's no sense in bearing grudges, keeping things to yourself and feeling hard done by. It's much better to talk about it and try and understand why things are as they are. That's something my gran taught me and she was right. You can't change the past. You've just got to come to terms with it.'

He was right of course, and that was what I was doing gradually. But it took time.

'I was adopted,' I said.

'So are a lot of people. They're not all unhappy. Is that what's bugging you?'

'Partly. I didn't get on too well with my parents and they didn't tell me till I happened to find out from an aunt, then they had to admit it.'

'That would be difficult to take,' he said with sympathy.

'That started me thinking and I couldn't understand why my real mother had wanted to get rid of me.'

'Must have been some reason,' said Daniel. 'I suppose

that was why you came south. To get away from them?'

'Yes.' I didn't want to go into it any further. 'Look, I must be going. I've got to get something ready for supper.'

'All right. I'll take you. I'll just go and tell Gran and close her window.' He came down a moment later, saying she was asleep.

He opened the door of the van and I got in.

'Thanks for getting the medicine, Judith, and for keeping an eye on Gran.'

'I'm fond of her,' I said.

As we set off, he said, 'I saw the Guvnor drop you off.'

'Yes. I went into Gatehurst with him. We stopped on the way and he went to see about the horses.'

'So he's made up his mind. I rather hoped it might blow over, but I suppose that was too much to hope. I wonder where he's selling them?'

I looked at him in surprise. 'Didn't you know? Surely he told you? He called in at the riding stables.'

He swore under his breath. 'No, he doesn't discuss anything with me. It's downright wicked to send animals like that to a riding school. They'll get all the heart knocked out of them. It's typical of him. He couldn't be bothered to find a decent home for them. If he'd asked me I'd have told him. I hear of plenty of chaps who could do with a couple of good horses, but I'm the last person he'd ask.'

'Does it matter very much, Daniel?' I tried to comfort him. 'They'll get fed and well looked after, even if they do have to work every day.'

'Half those people don't know one end of a horse from another and they pull their mouths about. They need old horses for that sort of work. But there's nothing I can do about it. Sometimes I think he does it to get at me.'

'Why? What does he want to do that for?'

'Because when I don't agree with him I say so. He's the sort of man who dislikes opposition.'

I could believe that and I thought that in future I would keep well clear of him. I wondered what had made him like that.

'Sometimes I feel sorry for him,' I said. 'Nobody seems to like him, except Mrs Carey and she has more reason to dislike him than anybody.'

'If you think that, you don't really know her. She simply can't see wrong in anyone. Unlike him, the accident has made a saint of her.'

'What was she like before, Daniel? Hasn't she always been like this then?'

'Oh, she was always pleasant, a good employer and all that, but the accident was what really changed her.'

'How? Do you mean her character suddenly changed?'

'Yes. I didn't really notice, but Gran said it was awful. She was very sick – in her mind as well as her broken body. Nobody knew what to do for her, least of all Mr Carey. I think Gran helped her as much as anyone at that time.'

'In what way?' This was quite a new image of my mother, one that I found very hard to visualize. I wanted to hear every detail.

'Gran used to talk to her, much like she did to me once. Told her it wasn't the end of the world. That people had come through worse things than that. In a nice way of course, and she took it from Gran.' He paused. 'It's funny to think that Gran herself is ill now. I can't remember when that last happened. She's always been the tower of strength to other people when they need her.' He was thoughtful for a moment, then he went on. 'I remember Gran saying that there was a gradual change in Mrs Carey. One day she asked Gran to go and buy her a Bible and it started then. I think she found something there she could rely on, someone who wouldn't let her down and could really help her. That's what Gran thinks anyway.'

'Do you believe it too, Daniel?'

He shrugged. 'I don't know what to believe, but I'm sure she's found something that's more important to her than her disability. Sometimes I think she's not even bothered she has to be in a wheelchair for the rest of her life.'

There wasn't time to say any more. We had reached the drive and Daniel swung the van into the yard. I got out and walked towards the house. As I reached the back door, Mr Carey came out. He saw Daniel driving off and then he looked at me. He didn't say a word but went across to the horses. I knew he was angry but it didn't bother me. I could only think of what Daniel had just told me.

Chapter Nine

The horses had gone and Daniel was like a bear with a sore head. I hadn't heard him whistling for days. Mr Carey had rung through one morning and said he had made arrangements for the horses to go and would Daniel have them ready. A couple of men from the riding school came and rode them back to the village.

'He didn't have the nerve to tell me himself, did he?' Daniel complained bitterly. 'I'm going to buy that mare back, if it costs me my last penny. I trained her myself and I'm not letting her go to a riding school.'

'Where will you keep her?'

'There's that stable at our place and I can get grazing for her on the farm. Keep that to yourself, though. I don't want to make trouble.'

I was glad that he trusted me enough to tell me.

On Saturday afternoon I decided to take the bike into the village to do some shopping. After lunch I went upstairs to my bedroom to change. I heard voices in the yard below. Since the horses had gone the yard was quiet and empty. Daniel was not often to be seen there, as though the empty boxes upset him, but now I recognized his voice and heard a girl's laughter.

I went over to the window and looked down to see Daniel with a grin on his face in conversation with a tall blonde girl. I couldn't see who she was as her back was turned but he seemed to know her well and obviously enjoyed talking to her.

I drew back from the window. I would have to wait till

they had gone as I was not going into the barn to get the bike while they were there. I changed into my jeans and sat down and waited.

Presently the voices stopped and I heard light footsteps coming towards the house. Then I heard the back door open. I went across to the window. Daniel had gone into the barn where I could hear him whistling. I went over to the mirror and tidied my hair, thinking that my short bob had improved my appearance. It gave my slightly upturned nose and brown eyes an impish look. Satisfied, I picked up my bag and went down to the kitchen. The girl was there, reading the newspaper on the kitchen table.

She looked up and said, 'Hullo. Who are you?'

'Judith. I work here,' I said. 'But I don't know you.'

'Sophie. I live here, at least I used to, but it's still my home. I'm their daughter.' She was very pretty with grey eyes and a strong likeness to her mother.

'Yes, of course. I've heard about you.'

'Good news, I hope? Is Mummy resting?'

'No, she's in the sitting room.'

'I'll go through. I didn't say I was coming, so she's not expecting me.'

I went out to get the bike from the barn. I was relieved to find that Daniel had gone. I didn't want to see him just then.

By the time I'd done the shopping and called in at Mrs Bill's on the way back it was almost dark. Daniel's van had gone. I went to find Mrs Carey in the sitting room.

'I didn't know your daughter was coming home this week-end,' I said.

'Neither did I,' she said, looking up from her book. 'I would have told you had I known. She's like that. Suddenly turns up without warning. But it's good to see her and I hope you'll get on well together.'

'Is she staying long?'

'Only for the week-end. She's out with friends at the

moment.' There had been no sign of the van at the cottage, either, and I wondered if she and Daniel were out together. The thought depressed me. I sat down in a chair opposite her and picked up my knitting.

'You're looking rather tired, Judith. Are you feeling all right, dear?'

'Yes, I'm fine. By the way, Mrs Bill sent her love. She hopes to be back at the end of next week.'

'Did the doctor say it would be all right? I know she hates being away.'

'She seems much better.'

'I've enjoyed our sessions in the kitchen,' said Mrs Carey. 'I don't know how I would have managed without you over the last few weeks, but you've had no time off. No wonder you're tired.'

I looked at her kind, concerned face. I'd grown so fond of her. Although it meant more work, I had enjoyed the time since Mrs Bill had been away, and I think it had been good for Mrs Carey too. We had moved the kitchen table up against the wall to make room for her chair and she helped me with the cooking. I prepared everything and together we tried out new recipes.

Nothing more had been said about my leaving. I dreaded the day they might tell me they had found a suitable person to take my place. I felt sure that when Mr Carey made that decision, as he did with the horses, my mother would accept it.

'I think, dear,' she broke in on my thoughts now, 'that when Mrs Bill returns, you should take a few days off. Go and see your parents. You must want to visit them and they'll be anxious to see you too.'

'I'd rather not,' I said.

'But why? The things which caused arguments when you were a child are passed. You're older now, a woman in your own right. You're free to come and go as you please.'

65

'Just the same, I would have to answer questions, ones I don't want to answer.'

'Don't they know you're working here?'

'No.'

'But why not, Judith?' She frowned. 'Surely they have a right to know. Haven't you written to them since you've been here?'

'Yes, but I didn't give my address.'

'Because you didn't want them to find you?'

I nodded. 'Not at present. I'll go back sometime.'

'You once told me you felt you hadn't been a very good daughter. Now is the time to put that right. I think you should go soon,' she urged. 'Please do it for me. I feel responsible for you, you know. After all I am your employer and I'm fond of you.'

I bent my head to hide the tears in my eyes. This sort of conversation upset me and instead of making it easier to tell her who I really was, it was becoming more difficult. I was afraid of what would happen if the truth was known and she found out that I had been deceiving her. Another thing was that when I thought of all those disagreements we used to have at home, I had a guilty feeling niggling at me. I knew that often it had been my fault. My parents' attitude had been uncompromising but sometimes I had aggravated it. Maybe one day I would go back and try to make amends.

'I know there's something troubling you,' she went on. 'It's as though you're afraid to talk about it. I don't want to pry but it might be better if you told me. I think it has something to do with your parents. That's why I believe, if you went back to them now, it might help you to straighten out your own feelings. Resentment, however justified, can only make us unhappy, even ill. Will you go, Judith? I would like to give you the fare.'

All my excuses had been swept away and I was too tired

to argue any more. And she might be right. Perhaps I should go home.

'All right,' I said without enthusiasm.

Early the next morning I awoke to the sound of piano-playing. I looked at my watch. It was seven-thirty. I was usually downstairs by seven but the night before it had been late before I fell asleep. I had heard the grandfather clock strike two and shortly afterwards a car drew up. The door slammed and then I recognized Sophie's voice. There was a roar of laughter which came from a number of people in the car and then a man's voice speaking. There were cries of 'Goodnight. See you soon', and the car revved up and drove off with a screech of wheels on the gravel.

I had heard Sophie come in at the back door, up the stairs to her room. She moved about for a long time and I was still listening to her when I dropped off to sleep.

Now, I got out of bed, dressed and went downstairs. Sophie was sitting at the piano, playing with what sounded to me like professional skill. Late nights didn't seem to affect her. She looked up as I passed the door.

'Hullo,' she said. 'Did I wake you?'

'No, I should have been up long ago. I didn't sleep very well last night.'

'We probably woke you when we came back. It was rather late.'

'No, I was reading a long time.'

'How long are you staying here?' was her next question.

'As long as your mother needs me.'

'You must get bored. I couldn't stand it. That's why I went away. And, of course, I wanted to study music which meant I had to go to London.'

'You play very well.'

'If you knew anything at all about music you'd say I haven't been practising nearly enough. In fact I'm likely

67

to fail my next exams unless I make up for it. It's not easy to get in all the hours I have to do at college and you can't practise when you're living in digs, like I am.'

'That must be difficult.'

'Also it rather interferes with my social life, but no doubt I'll scrape through.'

'Are you going to teach music?'

'Not if it's the last job on earth,' she said. 'I intend to be a concert pianist.' She ran her fingers over the keys and I was about to leave the room when she said, 'What do you do with your time off?'

'I usually find something to do. Walking, going into the village.'

'Do you ride?'

'No. I never learned.'

'Daniel would teach you. I expect he would be pleased to. He's quite good-looking, don't you think?'

I was annoyed by the question. 'There aren't any horses now, are there?' I said shortly. 'Besides I haven't the time.' I turned on my heel and went into the kitchen.

I wondered if she wanted to help her mother down that morning, but she hadn't said anything. I went upstairs to Mrs Carey's room. She was already dressed and waiting for me to help her into the wheelchair.

'How long are you staying, dear?' she asked Sophie at breakfast.

'Only till this evening. I'm meeting Daddy for dinner in town. I'll use this morning for practising and then go for a ride in the afternoon.'

'You know the horses have gone, don't you?' her mother asked.

'Yes. Daniel told me about them, but he knows of a couple we can borrow.'

I thought that, as she hadn't been down for some time and had to leave that evening, she might have spent more time with her mother, but obviously Sophie wasn't that sort of person. Daniel, too, had said something to that effect a while back.

Chapter Ten

I didn't tell Mum and Dad I was coming to see them. It wasn't likely they'd be away. I decided just to walk in on them and give them a surprise.

I took the bus from the station and got off at the end of our road. It seemed as though I had been away for ages, yet things hadn't changed. The same buses running to the same places; people coming out of the launderette; old Mr Taplin making for the *Blue Boar* and people going into the corner shop for their evening paper. It was just getting dark as I walked up the garden path. The lights were on, so somebody was at home.

For a moment I hesitated at the front door and then walked in.

'Mum!'

'Judith!' Mum came flying out of the kitchen and flung her arms round me. 'I didn't ever think you'd come back to us.'

I hugged her too. Now I was back home I had to admit I was pleased to see her, especially now I was sure of my welcome.

'Why didn't you tell us where you were?' Mum asked. 'We've been worried sick.'

'I did write and tell you I was all right.'

'Yes, but then nothing more and there was so much we wanted to know.'

She put her hands on my shoulders and looked at me. She seemed much older. She had always been a big woman but she had lost weight and it made her look shrunk and wrinkled.

'Are you all right, Mum?' I asked anxiously. 'Have you been ill?'

'Let's not talk about me now, dear. I'm perfectly all right now we've got you home again.'

'I can't stay long, Mum. I've got a job. Three days and then I must go back.'

'But why, Judith? Why can't you get a job round here?'

'I'll explain tonight when Dad gets back from work. I'll tell you what I'm doing and why I did it.' I would have to tell them. In a way I owed it to them.

After we'd been talking for a while, Mum said, 'I must phone Dad at the office. It would be too much of a shock for him to come home and find you here.'

'All right.' But she came back without speaking to him. 'He's already left. He'll be home in a few minutes.'

I was sitting facing the door when he came in. I saw him take off his coat in the hall. Mum sat opposite me. She didn't move and then Dad came in and saw me.

'Judith!' His words were the same as Mum's but his expression was very different.

I got up and went over to him, intending to kiss him, but he drew back .

'What brings you home, then?' he asked. There was no warmth in his voice.

'I came to see you and Mum.'

'You mean things haven't worked out for you so you've come home again.'

'Dad,' Mum protested.

I went back to my seat. 'No, Dad. I'm all right. I've got a job. I came back to see you and Mum.'

'Why should you suddenly feel concerned about us? You haven't given us a thought up to now. No telephone call, just a brief note with no address. How did you think your mother was feeling? It's made her proper poorly.'

'Dad, you mustn't speak to her like that. Not now's she's come back.'

He put out his hand as though to keep her out of the conversation.

'Let me handle this, Edith. You can't suddenly go off like that without a word and leave us worrying for months. Then you come home as though everything's the same as it's always been. It isn't. We might not have got along well together, but we've given you a good home and done the best we knew for you. We've *cared*. Maybe that's why we've been overstrict sometimes. And this is how you've repaid us. Frankly, I'm disgusted. It's been a bitter disappointment for me, I can tell you. And for your mother.'

I looked down to hide the tears which smarted my eyes. He was right. Every word of it was true and I would have to take it from him. I had nothing to say in my defence, only that I couldn't stand living with them a moment longer than I had to. I couldn't tell him that, but it was the truth and the reason I left. It was the reason I had to find my mother.

It all came back to me, the hostility, the pent-up feelings. I hadn't made a mistake. It was as inevitable as my growing up. But I was glad I had come back. We had to talk about it.

His outburst was followed by a silence which even Mum seemed unable to break. In fact, she was close to tears and her voice broke when she eventually said, 'Give over, Dad. This should be a happy occasion. Judith is only staying a few days before she goes back to work. Let bygones be bygones.'

'He's right, Mum. These things needed to be said, but now Dad has told me what he feels, I think I should tell you what I'm doing and why I did it.'

'Fair enough,' muttered Dad, sitting down in his armchair.

'You may be right, Dad,' I said slowly. 'I've probably been an awful disappointment to you. I *am* grateful for all you've done. Please believe that. But, perhaps because I'm adopted, I just can't see things the way you and Mum do. So often I thought you stopped me from enjoying myself just for the sake of it. You never seemed to understand that a young girl needs some freedom to be with her friends. Then, if I didn't toe the line, you tore me off a strip, treated me like a child when I was growing up and needing all the confidence I could get. I wanted encouragement and support so badly.'

'Now, steady on . . .'

'No, please Dad, let me go on. It's difficult enough to have to say what I·have to. I've always felt, well . . . different from you − as though I didn't really belong. And then when I found out that you had adopted me, I knew why. Gradually I began to wonder about my real mother and then when this new law came in which allowed children to trace their natural mother, my mind was made up. I was determined I would find mine one day.'

'Judith!' My mother had gone as white as a sheet. I wished I could have spared her this, but I knew I had to talk about it. 'Why didn't you tell us?'

'Because I was afraid you might try and stop me. I didn't even know whether I would succeed in finding her, but I did.'

I waited for a while, but they didn't interrupt me. Then I went on. 'The Social Services helped me and the adoption society and, with a little searching on my part, I found out where she lived.'

'But it must have been a terrible shock for her. Did you write to her first?' Mum asked.

'No. And that's why I can't tell you where she is or anything, because she doesn't know I'm her daughter.'

'But why? Why didn't you tell her?' Mum burst out.

73

'If you wanted to find her, why didn't you say who you were?'

'Because she isn't well and I don't feel I should tell her yet.'

'That doesn't seem fair to me,' Mum said. 'You know who she is and yet she doesn't know who you are. It will be a worse shock for her when she does find out. You're doing the same thing to her which you accused us of doing when we kept the facts about your adoption from you.'

'Sometimes it worries me,' I admitted.

'Where are you living?' asked Dad. 'Have you got a job?'

'Yes. I've got a living-in job. Helping in a big house.' I wasn't going to tell them I was living and working with my mother.

After supper Dad went up to bed and I went into the kitchen to make a cup of coffee for me and Mum.

As we sat drinking it, Mum said, 'You mustn't be upset with what Dad said. He's been that worried. He couldn't understand why you should want to go off and leave us.'

'It's true what he said. Perhaps it was selfish of me but I had to do it. In any case I'm nineteen now and I've got to make a life for myself. Even if I hadn't found my mother, I would still have gone off to find a job.'

'You didn't have to. A lot of children go on living and working from home until they get married. I must say, Judith, that you make me feel that we've failed terribly somewhere.' There were tears in her eyes.

I felt sorry for her. 'Look, Mum. Don't feel like that. It's just that I don't see things the way you and Dad do. Sometimes it's like that between parents and their children. Then it's best to go. I'll still keep in touch. I promise.'

She cheered up then. 'You'll write more often. You'll come and see us sometimes, then?'

'Yes, but at the moment I can't tell you where I'm

living. Give me time to get myself sorted out.'

She sighed and then said with an unsteady little laugh, 'I suppose we'll have to agree to that, shan't we? We haven't much say in the matter.'

'Let's leave it at that, Mum. Let's enjoy the next two days. You know I'm all right and that I'm doing what I want to do. And it must be better for you and Dad, not having me around arguing all the time.'

I went over and kissed her. 'I must go to bed now. I'm so tired. See you tomorrow.'

The next day after Dad had gone to work Mum and I went shopping. I needed a few new things and this time she seemed to enjoy helping me choose, without trying to force her own ideas on me. We treated ourselves to a cup of coffee in town and came home for lunch. In the afternoon I rang Annie, my old school friend. She sounded really pleased and said she was going to a party that evening with some of the old gang. Would I join them? I told her I'd like to.

'Do you mind, Mum? I would like to see Annie again.'

She put a brave face on it. Perhaps she was relieved that it avoided the possibility of Dad and me having words again.

When he came home, I could see that it was still on his mind, but he didn't get at me again. In fact he was nice to me and asked me about my job. I told him it was just housework and that I was learning to cook and what I was earning. He seemed to think that it was satisfactory. Mustn't let myself be put upon, he said. People are always ready to take advantage of you and if you don't have a trade union behind you, you could be in trouble.

I assured him I was treated very well and was given plenty of time off.

When he heard I was going out for the evening, he only said, 'I don't suppose you'll be late. We'll leave the door open and you can lock it when you come in.' Quite a concession for him.

Annie came round to pick me up. She was with a boy called Dave who we used to know at school, but I didn't know the other couple in the car. Once we got to the party there were a number of people there I remembered, though none of them well, except a boy called Steve. I went out with him for a while when we were at school – until Mum and Dad made it so difficult that it broke up. I didn't like him enough to go through all the fuss that went on at home.

Steve came straight up to me. 'Hullo, Judith. I thought you'd gone away for good.'

'I come back from time to time,' I said vaguely.

'It's good to see you again. You've changed. Your hair's different.'

'I had it cut off.'

'You look stunning. How long are you staying?'

'Till Monday.'

He frowned. 'That's not long.'

Half-way through the evening when everyone else was dancing he said, 'We've got some catching up to do. Meet me tomorrow?'

I shook my head. 'Sorry, Steve. I want to spend it with Mum and Dad. I don't often see them now.'

'Same old story? Why don't you do what *you* want? You're not a kid.'

'It's what I want.'

'Perhaps I can persuade you to change your mind. Let's go to the disco and make the most of this evening anyway.'

'No, Steve. It's good to see you again, but I came with Annie and I want to spend a little more time with her.'

He shrugged. 'OK. Why don't we wander out for a while and then come back? How about a kiss? Just for old times' sake, Judith?'

Annoyed that he kept on, I said, 'Look, I've got a rotten

headache. I'd much rather sit around with the others till they're ready to go home.'

'I'll run you home now if you're not feeling too good.' I should have thought of that one.

I got up and, disentangling myself from his arm which had slipped round my waist and which was already straying, walked back into the other room and sat down beside Annie.

'There you are,' she said. 'When am I going to see you again? I want to hear your news.'

I wanted to have time to talk to her. I needed to talk to someone badly, so I said, 'If I come round to your place tomorrow, just for an hour, will that be all right?'

'Of course. I'll be waiting for you.'

I wasn't back home late. Mum and Dad had gone to bed, thank goodness, and I locked the door and crept up to bed.

The next morning I went round to Annie's.

'I don't know if I should tell my mother,' I said, after I had told her all about my search. 'I get in such a muddle thinking about it. There's so much at stake.'

'Do you think she'll want you to go if you do?'

'I don't know.'

'I think she would,' said Annie. 'Rather than risk everyone else finding out. If she didn't mind them knowing, she'd have told them ages ago.'

'I think if the opportunity arises, I might, but the longer I leave it the more difficult it is to explain why I left it so long. It seems deceitful.'

'I think it is,' said Annie.

'Do you really? So long as I do my job properly, I don't think so. I can't suddenly come out with it. I've got to wait till I get an opportunity. Besides . . .' I was thinking of Daniel, but I wasn't prepared to tell her about that. What was there to tell anyway? That I was thinking of him all the time and that I was miserable because I thought he fancied Sophie?

'Besides what?'

'Nothing. It's just the fact that I like everyone there so much. I'd hate them to think badly of me.'

'Why should they? Anyway, it could be a secret between you and your mother. No one else need know.'

I was thoughtful. 'I don't know, Annie,' I said at last. 'It's not so easy and sometimes I'm scared. It's such an *important* thing, and I'm so afraid of handling it badly. The trouble is I *love* her.'

Annie looked at me, a puzzled expression on her face. 'It is a difficult situation, isn't it? You can hardly believe it's possible. In the end you'll have to decide for yourself, won't you?'

'I guess so. But thanks, anyway. It helps to talk about it.'

The rest of the day passed quietly, Dad reading his Sunday paper and working for a while in the garden, while Mum and I talked. Early on Monday morning I left.

Mum cried as she kissed me goodbye. 'Come home again soon,' she begged.

I said I would come when I could. But, for the time being, three days were enough. After Dad's outburst I knew it wouldn't work for longer.

Sitting on the train going south, I was sad about it, sad that all those years might have been happier for us all. But the clock couldn't be put back and, even if it could, we were the same people and things could never be different between us.

Chapter Eleven

I reached Gatehurst in the evening and took a taxi from the station. I found Mrs Bill in the kitchen doing some ironing. She had been back at work for a week now but I was shocked to see she had lost weight and didn't look well. She insisted that she was fit enough to work.

'I can't stand the boredom at home,' she said. 'Did you have a nice time, dear?'

'Yes, thank you,' I said politely, 'but it's nice to be back.'

'I've kept supper for you in the oven, but go in and see Mrs Carey first. She's missed you.'

My mother was reading in the sitting room. I was so pleased to see her that I went over and kissed her.

'You look better, dear. Much more rested. How are your parents?'

'Fine, thank you, but Mrs Bill doesn't look well.'

'I know. I'm worried about her. She's been sleeping here while you were away and she doesn't sleep well except in her own bed. Mrs Dawtry has promised to come more often and we'll help out where we can. But it's not easy with Mrs Bill She's touchy when other people take over her work. We'll have to be strict with her. I think she has something for your supper. Go and eat it, dear, then Daniel will run her home.'

I went back to the kitchen and ate my supper, while Mrs Bill put on her hat and coat. 'I'll be back at the usual time in the morning,' she said.

'Take it easy for a while, Mrs Bill. I'm sure Mrs Carey wouldn't mind if you came in later.'

'I shall come when I'm ready,' the old lady said, warning me against any further words of advice.

When I finished I washed the dishes. The kitchen was, as always, clean and tidy, so they had managed very well without me. I went back to my mother.

'Now, sit down, dear, and tell me about your time at home.'

I gave her a brief account, leaving out the bit about Dad's outburst, as I was afraid she would try and persuade me to go home more often. I could honestly say that I enjoyed seeing everyone again, but I preferred working down here.

'How were your parents? You said before things could be happier. I hope they were this time.'

'Yes, I think so. Mum was glad to see me, but Dad was a bit upset.'

'Because you left home?'

'Yes, partly. He said I'd been a disappointment to them. I can understand it in a way, but I thought he should know how I felt about it too, and when I told him, he was angry. We can never change our ideas on that, so it's best not to discuss it. It always leads to trouble.'

'It's no good to pretend the differences don't exist, either,' she said. 'You could be the one to change your ideas, Judith, if you wanted to. I think you'd find that your father would come more than half-way to meet you then.'

'But why should I?' I protested. 'Mum's all right, but Dad made me miserable sometimes. I can't forget that.' I had tried to avoid telling her about it, but now she had pressed me, I was angry. Angry with Dad and his attitude, angry that my own mother couldn't understand what I had to put up with. 'I don't want to talk about it any more,' I said. 'Tell me what you've been doing.'

'You might think that I've no right to offer my opinion on this, dear, but you need to talk and express your feelings, otherwise it's like a poison that festers in your mind. You won't be happy until you can forgive whatever it is that you condemn in your father.'

I said nothing. What she was suggesting was impossible, and she had no right to expect it of me because she was the cause of it in the first place. But it didn't stop me loving her and I hated this disagreement between us. It was the first time I had been near to having an argument with her and I felt miserable. Even at this distance, it seemed that Dad had some sort of influence on my life.

My mother was smiling at me. 'Come on, Judith, don't look so stubborn. I know how difficult it is, but it can be done. There, let's not talk about it any more now. It's past my bedtime, so if you wouldn't mind helping me . . .'

As I helped her undress she told me what she had been doing since I was away.

'I've started another picture. I found an old photograph of the harbour. Now I've got the outlines I want to go down sometime and have a look at it on a sunny afternoon. I think now that the days are warmer, we'll ask Daniel to get the trap out. You'll enjoy that.'

It was good to hear her planning her days. She looked so happy and I was glad that in that moment of anger, I'd said nothing to cause her distress. I knew I was right in keeping my secret from her anyway for a little longer.

The next morning I went out to ask Daniel for some vegetables for dinner. He was washing down the car.

'Have a good time?' he asked.

'Yes, thanks.'

'What did you do?'

'I went to see my folk.'

He picked up the bucket and threw the rest of the water over the bonnet. 'What kind of vegetables do you want?' he asked.

'Leeks and broad beans if they're ready, Mrs Bill said.'

I followed him into the kitchen garden, carrying a basket.

'I thought you didn't care much for going home,' he said.

'I don't, but Mrs Carey thought I should go and let them know how I was getting on. I'm glad I did.'

'Worked out all right, then?'

He was looking at me and suddenly I wanted to tell him the truth. 'No, as a matter of fact, it didn't. It was no better than before. Dad gave me a piece of his mind.'

'What about?' He began pulling the leeks, cleaning off the dirt and putting them in the basket.

'Leaving home like I did. Without telling them.'

'Is that right?' He straightened up and looked at me. 'Sounds a bit drastic.'

'I had to leave. I was never happy there and I couldn't do what I wanted.'

'Yes, I remember. You came to look for someone, but you don't ever go out much. So I reckon it's someone near here. Am I right?'

I hesitated. I was on dangerous ground, yet I felt that with Daniel my secret would be safe. If I didn't tell him, he'd get it out of me anyway. He had an uncanny habit of alighting on the truth.

'If I tell you, will you promise not to tell anyone?'

'No,' he said. 'I can't do that. If it's something that I think I ought to bring to someone's notice, I won't be bound by promises.'

'Then I won't tell you,' I flared. 'If you can't keep a confidence you're not much of a friend.'

He stopped digging the leeks and straightened. 'Look, Judith, if you're in any sort of trouble, I'd like to help you, but I can't make promises that would stop me acting for the best. I have an idea it's something to do with Mrs Carey, but I wouldn't want anything to upset her.'

'Neither would I!' I hissed at him. 'I love her. She's my mother.'

He let out a long slow whistle. 'So that's it. The thought crossed my mind, but it just didn't make any sense.'

'Why not? Am I so very different from her?'

'No,' he said slowly. 'No, it's not that. If you'd gone to all this trouble to find her, why didn't you tell her?'

'Because I didn't think she'd let me stay. Then I thought I should get to know her better before I asked all the questions that have been bothering me for years.'

'And have you found the answers?'

'Not by any means. And I don't suppose I will till she knows who I am.'

'How did you find her?'

I told him the long story.

'Did they tell you she couldn't walk?'

'No, and when I found out for myself that was another reason why I kept quiet. It would have been such a shock when she seemed to be at a disadvantage.'

'Do you really think she doesn't know already?'

'Of course she doesn't. How could she? She knows I was adopted, but nothing else. Not even my name would mean anything to her.'

'Just the same, you *were* adopted and you're about the age her daughter would be if she . . .'

'Got rid of me,' I finished for him.

'You *are* bitter, aren't you?'

I didn't answer. I felt like crying. I bit my lip and bent down, pretending to pick the beans. But he came and stood in front of me and lifted my chin with gentle fingers, so that I was forced to look at him. His eyes were sympathetic as he brought out a handkerchief and handed it to me. 'Poor Judith. What a secret to keep to yourself all this time.'

'You won't tell her, will you, Daniel?' I begged.

'No, I won't. Something like that is for you to speak of

83

in your own time. If it is news to her, I have a feeling it won't be unwelcome. She's very fond of you. You'll let me know, won't you, when you break it to her?'

'Yes, I will.'

'I wonder what the Guvnor would say if he knew.'

'He'd sack me straight away.' I was sure of that.

'Come on,' said Daniel, suddenly matter-of-fact. 'Let's get these beans picked.'

As I walked back to the house with the basket full of fresh vegetables, I felt incredibly light-hearted. The old saying was true — that a burden shared was a burden halved. I trusted Daniel and I knew he wouldn't let me down. He didn't blame me either. In fact he seemed to understand how difficult it was.

Mrs Carey was in the kitchen talking to Mrs Bill when I came in. 'It's such a lovely day,' she said. 'I think it would be a good idea to go out in the trap this afternoon. If you learned to drive, Judith, I can see no reason why we shouldn't be able to go out together now the summer's coming. It would be very pleasant.'

After lunch Daniel harnessed Joey and we brought Mrs Carey out in her light chair. He had thought of an ingenious way of wheeling her up into the trap by means of planks and then strapping her to the seat so that she could not slip. He put a rug over her knees and tucked it round her. The chair was then folded and put under the seat in case we needed it.

Then Daniel got in and picked up the reins and I sat beside him. Joey was a tough good-natured pony and had no difficulty pulling the trap with its big rubber wheels. So we set off down the drive. Once on the straight narrow road, Daniel lifted the reins, bringing them down on the pony's back and, with ears pricked, Joey broke into a smart trot.

The regular clip-clop of hooves as the trap swayed along the leafy lane; the movement of Daniel's body close to me and my mother's happy chatter all seemed to make it one of the happiest moments of my life. I was with the two people I cared for more than anyone else in the world and, just then, I felt sure that everything would turn out right without any effort on my part. I should have known that I could not expect to walk into people's lives with knowledge that would disrupt their very existence, without causing distress. But that afternoon such thoughts were far from my mind.

On the way back, Daniel asked if I would like to take over the driving. I changed places with him and he told me how to hold the reins with just enough pressure to feel the pony's mouth. He told me how to move across first to one side of the road, then to the other. I soon got the hang of it and was thrilled to find how Joey responded to my guidance on the reins.

When we got back, I settled Mrs Carey in the house and went out to help Daniel unharness the pony. I wanted to learn so that I could do it myself.

'I've bought the chestnut mare back,' he said. 'Would you like to see her?'

There was nothing to be done in the house at present so I drove back to the cottage with him. There, in the loose box at the end of the garden, was Fleet. She whinnied as we approached.

'She's beautiful, Daniel. Did she cost a lot?'

'A good deal less than she was sold for. They found she was no good for school work. She's bolted twice and they wanted to be rid of her quickly. I do some work for the owner from time to time when he's short of help, so he let me have her cheap. I still owe something on her but she's worth it.'

'Does Mr Carey know?'

'Not yet, but I expect he will soon enough. There's nothing he can do about it though. Mrs Carey knows. I told her what I intended to do and she thought it was all right. She knows I trained that mare myself and I'm the one who rides her most often. John's a good rider, too, and he knows how to handle her. He can take her out when he's home.'

'What about Sophie?'

'I'd never let her ride this mare. She's not good enough and she's too impatient with the animals.'

He rubbed the white blaze on the mare's nose and she nuzzled him. I understood her feeling of confidence in him. I felt the same.

Chapter Twelve

Mr Carey had not been home for two weeks. We were told he had gone to France. I'm sure Mrs Carey was unhappy on these occasions. Sometimes he phoned her or turned up unexpectedly but I wished she could count on regular visits as it would be something for her to look forward to. But even when he came he often spent the time working or making telephone calls.

Each day I tried to arrange a programme with her. Either we would go out for a drive, or for a ride in the trap and she spent a lot of time painting. I thought her pictures were good enough to sell, but she wouldn't hear of it.

I had not seen much of Daniel, either. Now he had his own horse to look after and Mrs Bill said he was helping out at the stables, I guessed he was anxious to get home as soon as he had finished his work.

Sophie came down for a few days. She spent most of the time practising the piano as her exams were coming up shortly. Usually she ignored me and I hardly ever saw her sitting down talking to her mother. In the evenings when she was not out with friends, she switched on the television which left little opportunity for conversation.

Sometimes she went riding with Daniel who managed to borrow a horse for her to ride. They usually left in his van, presumably to go to his cottage, and when they came back afterwards, Sophie seemed in no hurry to come indoors, but stood talking to him in the yard. When I heard their voices and laughter I thought how they enjoyed each other's company. When I was with Daniel we seemed to be struggling with a problem. It was depressing.

One Saturday at lunch Sophie announced that she was returning to London for a party that evening and that she was going for a ride before she left. 'Daniel's going to bring the horses round here to save time,' she said.

'I'd rather they didn't come here,' said her mother. 'Your father has sold the horses. If Daniel has bought one back, that's his business, but I'd rather they were kept away from here. It would only annoy your father if he knew.'

'But he won't. It will give me more time for piano practice. That's why we arranged it.'

'Very well,' said Mrs Carey with a sigh. 'But don't bring them back here afterwards. Take them straight back where they came from.'

I was in the kitchen washing up the lunch things when I heard Daniel ride into the yard. He was on Fleet and leading a dark brown horse.

Sophie was practising in the sitting room, ready dressed in her riding breeches. Her long fair hair hung loose over her shoulders and she looked very attractive. I could have told her that Daniel was waiting, but I didn't. He would have to come and ask me, I thought angrily. He dismounted and led the horses to the back door.

'Judith? Could you tell Sophie I'm ready?'

'All right.' I went through and told her. She hardly looked up from her playing and it was another five minutes before she came out.

Daniel was having some difficulty holding the two animals which appeared to dislike each other. Eventually he hitched Fleet's reins over a post and brought the other horse to the door ready for Sophie.

I heard their conversation clearly through the open window.

'Let me ride Fleet today.'

'No.'

'Why not? You never let me ride her.'

'And certainly not today. She's excitable since she's been back. I can't risk her bolting. It would ruin her and wouldn't do you much good either.'

Ignoring him, she walked over to where Fleet was standing. Daniel watched her but I don't think he saw what she had in mind. Unhitching the reins, she swung herself onto the mare's back, and turning to laugh at Daniel, she started off down the lane. I heard him swear. There was nothing for him to do but mount the other horse and go after her. Soon they were out of sight.

I turned away from the window with a sigh. Daniel might be angry but she was challenging him, and he wasn't one to turn his back on a challenge. And what if she managed Fleet all right, proved that she could ride her? Daniel would admire her for that.

I went into the sitting room. Mrs Carey was finishing off a painting she had started early in the spring. The colours were different now, but when I looked at the picture, every detail of the early spring scene was vivid.

'You should put on an exhibition. You have quite a few now.'

'No. Maybe one day, but I'm not satisfied yet.' She was a perfectionist but I was pleased that she was taking so much more interest in life. I liked to think it had something to do with me. Perhaps it was a vain dream to hope that she would get better, but I felt that if she was happy and purposeful, then it could only be good for her.

She looked up from her easel. 'Have they gone?'

'Yes. They set off just now.'

'Sophie's so much keener on riding these days,' she said. 'You know she disliked it as a child. It was only because John was so good at it and she didn't want him to have a pony to himself.'

'It's a pity now that the horses have gone.'

She laughed. 'That's Sophie all over. Once something becomes inaccessible she wants it. She'll learn sooner or later, poor Sophie.'

I didn't want to go on talking about Sophie.

'I thought Mr Carey was coming home this week-end,' I said.

'He said he might, but he would have been here by now. There's a business dinner on tonight which he might have to go to. It's for wives, too, though of course I can't go.'

'Do you mind very much?' I asked her.

She smiled, a little sadly. 'For Harry's sake, yes, but I never cared for business gatherings myself. Sophie goes with him sometimes.'

'I know he's busy, but I wish he'd spend more time with you.'

'He comes when he can. I wouldn't want him to come because he felt he ought to.'

'I think it's selfish. I think men are like that. All the ones I know anyway.'

'Of course they're not,' she said firmly. 'He used not to be like that.'

'Then why now? He should be much kinder to you after what happened.'

'Hush, Judith. You should never say that. The fact is that he can't forgive himself and that's a lot to do with it.'

'But if you don't blame him, why should he blame himself, specially if it makes you hate him?'

'Who said anything about hate?' she asked, looking at me. 'I love him.'

I stared at her. How could you go on loving someone so uncaring?

'I don't believe it,' I burst out. 'I couldn't love someone like that.'

'You'll understand when you love someone yourself. Unfortunately you can't choose who you fall in love with.

90

But I assure you if it makes you feel any better, I've never regretted it. On the whole I've been happy.'

'Even now?'

'Yes. I admit there have been times in my life when I've been very unhappy, but that happens to most people and perhaps if we feel the bad times keenly, we can enjoy the good times all the more.'

'I wish I had your way of looking at things,' I said.

I watched her as she picked up her brush and began mixing the colours on her palette. I thought she had forgotten about me, but presently she asked, 'Do you ever read the Bible, Judith?'

I shook my head. 'What good would that do?'

'Perhaps not much to begin with. But you'd soon find a lot of valuable help in it.'

'What do you mean? What kind of help?'

'We can't change ourselves into the sort of people we'd like to be. We need help over that and it's there for the asking. The Bible tells us that Jesus can change us. He can change our feelings and guide us through difficult situations if only we'd give him the chance.'

'I don't think he'd be very interested in someone like me,' I said. 'You have to be a good person for him to want to do anything about you. I can understand him wanting to help you.'

She laughed then. 'You've got it wrong, dear. None of us are good, but he loves us all the same and he wants us to depend on him. It's worth trying, you know.'

I shrugged. 'I don't really think I could. Not suddenly, like that. I'm not used to it.'

'It may seem strange at first, perhaps. But there are plenty of people, who get along for years without giving it a thought, then one day something happens and they realize they do need something more in their life, someone they can trust, someone who really cares about them.'

'It sounds all right,' I said reluctantly, 'but I don't feel like that. I admit I would like to change a lot of things about myself, but not that way. Besides I don't think it's all my fault I'm like I am.'

We might have gone much deeper into the subject, but we heard a car coming up the drive. Looking out of the window I saw Mr Carey pull up in front of the house.

'There he is, after all,' said my mother, putting away her paints.

I went into the kitchen as he came through the front door. Perhaps on this occasion he would give her a little more of his time. I had put the kettle on, intending to make them a pot of tea, when I heard galloping hooves coming down the lane and Fleet, without a rider and dragging reins, came clattering into the yard.

My only thought at the moment was to get the horse out of the way before Mr Carey discovered it, or it would spoil another week-end.

I ran across the yard as the mare, seeing the door of her box standing open, went in. I closed both doors so that she could not be seen from outside.

So Sophie had got her just reward and Fleet had bolted. I couldn't suppress a feeling of satisfaction, though I didn't want anyone to be hurt. Then it occurred to me that perhaps they needed help. I was about to set off when Mr Carey came out.

'I thought I heard horses,' he said.

'I don't think so,' I said.

He looked across the yard to where I had closed the doors. If only Fleet would stay quiet.

'I was just going to make tea,' I said, in an effort to get him back in the house.

But the mare was upset and nervous at being shut

in the dark stable and clattered around in her box. Mr Carey walked across and opened the door, and I followed him. Fleet was breathing hard and her neck was dark with sweat.

'What's this animal doing here?' He turned on me. 'Do you know anything about it?'

'She's just come into the yard. I don't know what happened.'

'Who was riding her?'

There was no point in lying. 'Daniel and Sophie went out earlier.'

'The horse was sold. How the devil did it get here?' He was shooting questions at me as though I was to blame and I didn't know what to say. 'Please ask Mrs Carey,' I said. She would know how best to answer him.

'There's not time now. Someone might be hurt. Go back in and I'll see if I can find them. Which way did they go?'

I pointed down the lane. Mr Carey led Fleet out of the stable and mounted her. He was still in his dark town suit, and his face was grim as he urged her into a trot.

I went back into the sitting room and explained what had happened. There was nothing to do but wait. It was another hour before they were back. Sophie came in limping and collapsed into a chair. She looked pale and her face was scratched.

'That vicious animal threw me,' she complained, feeling a swollen ankle. 'I can't possibly go to the party tonight now. I only hope it's not broken.'

'It won't be, dear, or you couldn't walk on it,' said her mother. 'We'll bind it up tonight and if it's worse tomorrow, you'll have to see the doctor.'

It was a long time before Mr Carey came in. When at last he did, he said nothing about the horses. A few minutes later I heard them leaving the yard and, through the window, I saw Daniel riding Fleet and leading the brown horse down the drive.

Chapter Thirteen

The household took several days to recover from the riding incident. Nothing more was said in front of me about the horses but there was a gloomy atmosphere for the rest of the week-end and even my mother was preoccupied. Sophie's leg was not broken but it was still very swollen and painful when Mr Carey took her back to London on Sunday.

Then John came home and, as always when he was about, the house was cheerful again.

Wednesday was my mother's birthday. We all had breakfast together and there was a pile of presents on the table. John gave her some new paint brushes and Sophie and Mr Carey had left presents for her. There were gifts, too, from Daniel and Mrs Bill and the postman brought cards. I had gone into the village the day before to buy her a book about flowers, illustrated by paintings. It was rather more than I could afford but I knew she would love it.

'I want you to write in it, Judith,' she said, handing the book to me. I spent some time thinking of the right words, words that I wished I could write. Anything less seemed worthless. I handed it back to her. 'Give me time to think,' I said.

Her birthday seemed to bring us all closer together and banish any unhappy feelings left over from the previous week-end. In the middle of the morning when I was helping Mrs Bill decorate the birthday cake, the front door bell rang. I went to open it.

A man stood there, holding a spray of red roses. 'These are for Mrs Carey.' I took them from him and read the card, 'To my dear wife, wishing you a happy birthday. With all my love, Harry.'

I went to find her. 'Look!' I said. 'These are for you.'

Her eyes lit up as she took them from me and read the note. 'From Harry,' she said. 'He never forgets my birthday. Judith, please bring me a vase and the secateurs.'

'Was that the florist with Mrs Carey's flowers?' asked Mrs Bill when I went into the kitchen. 'He never forgets.'

I took a vase and the secateurs back into the sitting room and watched as she arranged them. 'Such a lovely scent,' she said softly, laying the petals against her cheek.

What a strange man he was. One moment he was upsetting the whole family and the next, and it could only be because he loved her, he sent her red roses on her birthday.

I was surprised when Mr Carey came down again the following Friday afternoon. My mother had gone upstairs for a rest and I was in the kitchen. He came and asked me to come into the sitting room as he wanted to talk to me.

'Judith, I've been meaning to talk to you for some time about this. You've looked after my wife well, but you were employed on a temporary basis. The time has come now when I'm making other arrangements. As you know, Mrs Bill hasn't been well and I'm having to spend a good deal more time abroad and for longer periods. It's my intention to employ an experienced woman with nursing experience to look after my wife. I've now found the ideal person and she will be free to come in a week's time. This will give you a few days to make other arrangements.'

I was astounded. 'But does Mrs Carey know? She hasn't said anything to me about this.'

'Of course I shall discuss it with her. She'll be sorry to see you go but, for my own peace of mind, I'm forced to make a change and have arranged for her care on a more permanent basis. The responsibility is too much for you to shoulder when I'm out of the country and besides, certain things have been happening lately which confirms my opinion that we need an older woman in charge. My wife is not able to see all that goes on when she's confined to her chair.'

'But I thought I would have more warning. It's so sudden,' I protested.

'It's better that changes like this should be made quickly. Of course you will be well compensated. I intend to pay you a full month's salary and that should cover any expenses you might have.'

There was nothing I could say. He was, after all, within his rights. I knew this job could not last indefinitely but I had been so happy and I was certain I was good for Mrs Carey. I had not expected this curt dismissal.

It was no good arguing with him. There was nothing more to say. I had to get away and think about it, but at the door I stopped.

'But why didn't Mrs Carey tell me? She was the one to employ me.'

He didn't reply so I stumbled blindly into the hall and out of the back door. I had to get away from the house. I had no idea where I was going but I wanted to be alone while I tried to understand what had happened. I turned off the road onto a forest path.

I would have to leave. I had no choice. I already knew Mr Carey well enough to be sure that he would not change his mind even under pressure from his wife. I was certain she knew nothing about it. If she had, she would have warned me.

Where was I to go? I dreaded the thought of going back to live with my Mum and Dad. Dad might not even want me, but what was the alternative? I had managed to save a little money but not much and jobs were hard to come by. There was little enough time to make any arrangements. I had no idea what I ought to do. Whatever decision I made, the future seemed bleak.

I walked under tall green beeches until I came out of the wood onto open moor where the heather was beginning to bloom, covering the earth with purple. I wondered what Mr Carey would have said if I had told him about my mother, but that I could never do.

I followed some ponies deeper into the forest. There were no paths here and their hooves cracked and broke the dead wood fallen from the trees. Nervous because I had followed them, they broke into a trot and were soon out of sight. I stood alone in the wood, the big oaks and beeches towering over me and now I was afraid. I felt the aloneness and knew I would have to face it again soon in my own life. I had been very lonely in the past, but here I had forgotten about it. How insecure life was. Just when I thought I was making out all right, it was suddenly all snatched away. One moment I had a job and friends, the next I was back at the point where I started out. Was there no one I could trust?

It was then that I remembered what my mother had said about Jesus. If it was really true that he loved me and could help me through a difficult situation, I had nothing to lose by asking. I stood in the wood with the sunshine flickering through the leaves and I tried to find the right words. I had never prayed before, really prayed, I mean. I didn't count the set prayers when I occasionally went to church or at school. This was quite different. Here I was talking directly to Jesus, except that he didn't seem to be there. How could you talk to someone unless you could see them, or at least hear their reply?

As I stood there, struggling with my thoughts, I gradually felt incredibly peaceful and presently I sank to my knees in the seclusion of the trees and said softly, 'Please, Jesus, forgive me that I have never thought much about you before. I know now that I was wrong, but I never really felt the need. Now I need you desperately. I don't know what I should do. Please help me.'

I remained there for some time, the tears streaming down my cheeks. I had been given no sudden direction or guidance, but I was overwhelmed by the feeling that someone was sharing my burden, someone was here, right now, beside me and although I couldn't see him, I knew that I was no longer on my own.

I looked at my watch. It was seven o'clock. If I went back to the house now I would have to face everyone. I couldn't bear that.

I started to wander back and after a while found that I was going in the direction of Mrs Bill's cottage. She said I could drop in at any time and I could be sure she would ask no questions. I just hoped that Daniel would be out.

When I reached the cottage I saw with relief that Fleet was not in her stable. I knocked on the back door and walked in. Mrs Bill looked up from a magazine she was reading, pleasure on her face.

'Hullo, dear. You don't usually come round on a Friday. What is it?' She looked closely at me and I was afraid she could see I had been crying.

'Nothing really. Can I stay a while and talk? I just felt I wanted to get out.'

'Of course. As a matter of fact, I'm glad you came. I wanted to talk to you.'

'Why?' Surely they hadn't told her already I was leaving?

'It's nothing urgent. Put the kettle on, dear, and let's have some tea.'

I did as I was told and waited until it boiled. Then I put the tea on a tray and carried it over to her.

'I went to see the doctor the other day,' she said. 'He says I've got to ease up. I just wanted to tell you that I'm glad you're with Mrs Carey. It makes it easier to leave, knowing she's in your capable hands. Of course, I shall keep on coming over and help whenever I can be useful, but Mrs Dawtry will come every day now instead of just three days a week.'

'Have you told Mrs Carey?' I asked.

'I've mentioned it to her. Said I'll have to be thinking about it, but there's no hurry.'

'What did she say?'

'Said she'd been worrying about me. Thought I wasn't looking too well and that I should take things easy. With you and Mrs Dawtry, we'll manage.'

'Does Mr Carey know?

'I expect she's told him, but so long as things run smoothly in the house, he won't bother.'

There was a clatter of hooves outside, and I couldn't ask her any more.

'I'm glad he's back,' said Mrs Bill. 'I don't know why he's so late. Been out for hours with that mare.'

'I'd best be going then. He'll want his supper.'

'Why don't you stay, Judith? Have a bite of something with us.'

I was hungry and the stew on the stove smelt delicious. I was tempted. Then the door opened and Daniel came in and flung his jacket on the chair.

'You're here, then.' He looked at me accusingly. 'I've been out in the forest looking for you.'

'Me? Why?'

'You're usually back at the house by now, aren't you? Mrs Carey was bothered about you and asked me to go out and look.'

'I'm sorry. I went for a walk and have only just come back.'

'You could have told someone you were going instead of having them all worried.'

'Mrs Carey was resting when I left so I didn't see her. I'm going back now anyway,' I said, walking to the door.

'Hold on, I'll walk back with you,' said Daniel, and he picked up his jacket.

As we turned into the road he said. 'You've been crying. What's up? Why did you go off like that?'

'Mr Carey told me that I was to go. They don't need me any more.'

'What?' He stopped and, gripping my arm till it hurt, swung me round to face him.

'Why did he do that?' he demanded. 'Did he find out about your mother?'

I pulled loose. 'No. I haven't said anything. He said he wants an older person to look after her, specially when he's away a lot.'

'But Mrs Carey won't agree to it. She needs you.'

'They took me on temporarily and if he says so, she won't disagree with him. I don't want her to. I'd hate to be the cause of more arguments between them. I'd rather go without a fuss.'

'Maybe you're right,' he said thoughtfully, 'but it's going to upset her anyway. You've done nothing wrong and besides . . .'

'Besides what?'

He turned off the road and taking my hand, led me into the forest.

'Come on, there are things we've got to talk about even if it is late. I haven't had a chance to talk to you for days.'

'It's not my fault.'

He smiled at me. 'I didn't say it was.' He held my hand firmly as though he thought I might resist. 'Now,' he said, finding a patch of grass under an oak tree and sitting down with his back against it, 'let's talk about this. It seems incredible to me. You've been living in the same house as your own mother for six months now and nothing's been said by either of you. I would have thought some questions would have been asked which would have brought the subject to light.'

'Perhaps in the beginning, but not recently,' I said.

'If it meant so much to you to find your mother, why are you going away now without asking why she had you adopted? Don't you want to know any more?'

I was sitting beside him, my legs curled under me. I picked up a handful of dry earth and watched it trickling through my fingers.

'No,' I said softly. 'I love her and I can't ask her. Not now.'

'I understand your reasons, but I don't think you're right.' He paused. 'So, what are you going to do now?'

'I intend to go when they want me to.'

'Where?'

'I don't know. Back home, I suppose.'

'You hated it there. Why go where you'll be miserable and perhaps unwelcome?'

'There's nowhere else. Besides I have a feeling I must go back.'

'You could move in with Gran and me.'

How lovely that would be. That, surely, would be the answer to all my problems and what I wanted more than anything. But almost immediately, I knew it wouldn't work. How could I live in the Careys' cottage when I was no longer employed by them?

'I wish I could,' I said to him, 'but what would I do all day if I wasn't needed in the house? I must go and find a job somewhere else.'

'Something will turn up. You could look round locally.'

I shook my head.

'If you're short of money,' Daniel went on, 'I'll lend you some until you find a job.'

'Thanks, Daniel. That's really great, but I can manage. Besides you've got Fleet to pay for still.'

He grinned. 'I'd like to help though,' he said.

'You have. I'm clearer in my own mind what I must do.'

It was true. I felt certain now that I must go back home.

102

I got up. 'I must go back now. It's late.'

'Before you go, there's something I've been wanting to do for a long time.' He slipped his arms round my waist and drew me close to him until I could feel his heart beating. I couldn't resist him nor did I want to. My legs felt weak as he took me in his arms. As his lips touched mine, I closed my eyes as I responded to his kisses.

'I don't want you to leave, Judith. Can't you see?'

'How could I when you never told me?' I asked. I couldn't believe he felt the same way as I did. He had never shown his feelings at all. Besides I had always thought there was Sophie. I searched his face, longing for it to be true.

'I thought it was pretty obvious,' he said. 'Whenever I was about to say something you always rushed off. I thought you didn't *want* to hear.'

'I had no idea,' I said, looking into his eyes and seeing there a reflection of his words. 'If I'd known . . .'

'You must be blind.' His eyes crinkled at the corners as he smiled. 'Anyway, what difference would it make?'

'Just that I would have been so happy. Now it's too late.'

'Too late for what? It's never too late to tell you I love you. And I may be able to persuade you to stay now.'

I shook my head. 'I can't. I must go home.'

He reached for my hands and pulled me towards him again. 'Give me one good reason.'

I pulled away. 'I don't want to go. I don't want to leave you or my mother or anyone. But I've got to. Please don't make it more difficult.'

How could I explain to him that since that desperate moment in the woods, there really was someone taking charge of my life, urging me to do things which I didn't even want to do, but with such certainty that I had to obey?

I turned and ran towards the road, my mind in turmoil. Any other time his kisses would have been bliss, but now they only made it harder to leave. It was so unfair. He called after me, but I didn't look back.

Chapter Fourteen

The grandfather clock struck ten as I let myself in at the back door. The lights were still on in the sitting room but I didn't want to go in. I closed the door and went through to the hall.

'Judith, is that you?' It was my mother's voice. It was unusual for her to be up so late.

'Yes, Mrs Carey,' I called. 'Goodnight.' I started up the stairs.

Mr Carey appeared at the door. 'Judith, will you come in for a moment? My wife has something to say to you.'

Reluctantly I turned back to the sitting room. Everyone looked at me as I came in. Then John went over and turned off the television. My mother was sitting in her high-backed chair and for some reason Sophie was there too. She must have made a late decision to come home.

They waited for me to sit down.

'I'm sorry I wasn't there for supper,' I said. 'I went out.' It couldn't be because of this that everyone was looking so serious, but I felt that some explanation was due from me.

'There is something that I want to tell you all,' said my mother. 'We've been waiting for you to come back so that what I have to say will be heard for the first time by you all, although you, Judith, already know what I have to say.' She looked very pale, and her hands were gripping the arms of her chair as though whatever she was about to disclose was not going to be easy for her. 'I hope that when I tell you Judith is my daughter, you will receive it with compassion and accept her with love.'

There was absolute silence. I looked round at the faces and they were all looking at me . Then John came over and stood beside me. He seemed shocked and unable to take it in, but managed to blurt out, 'I always thought there was something special about you.'

Sophie got up and, without a word, left the room. Now there was Mr Carey. How would he take it? He went over to the bar and poured himself a drink.

My mother went on, looking at me, 'My husband, of course, knew of your existence, but he didn't know it was you who had come to look after me.'

'And you,' I asked, my voice little more than a whisper. 'When did you know?'

'From the day you came. In a way I expected you, but I will tell you about that tomorrow. All I want to say now, Judith, is that I'm glad you came. I never intended to tell you that I knew who you were. You wanted to find me and it had to be you who spoke first. I wanted to give you time to think about it and I hoped that in the meantime we could learn to know one another better.What surprised me was that you kept quiet for so long. But now that new arrangements have to be made, partly because of Mrs Bill's illness, I can't keep the secret any longer. You are my daughter and I will not give you notice. The time has come when everyone is entitled to know. That was why I asked Sophie to come down.'

Mr Carey stood with his back to the empty fireplace, a half-filled glass in his hand. For a moment I felt sorry for him, then I saw the anger in his eyes when he looked at me.

'You should have told me earlier, Isobel,' he said to his wife.

'I couldn't. You suddenly told me that you had engaged a housekeeper who was to start next week and that you had told Judith she must leave. You gave me very little time or choice in the matter.' For once my mother's voice was cold.

'You were probably right, though,' he said reluctantly. 'I don't think you could have done it any other way. But it puts a new complexion on what I said this afternoon. You're no longer an employee, Judith.' There was no warmth in his voice when he said this and his eyes were hostile. 'You're part of the family and as far as you are concerned, your mother must decide the best thing to do.'

'Judith and I will have to talk it over,' said my mother.

'Nevertheless I'd like to be consulted.' He turned to me. 'In my opinion you should have spoken up long before this. You can see now how embarrassing it is for all of us. What you did was deceitful and I, for one, will take a long time to get used to the idea.'

'I'm sorry.' I meant it. 'I wanted to avoid anything like this. That's the reason why I found it difficult to say anything.'

'How did you find us?' Mr Carey asked.

'Through the Social Services. And the adoption society helped. There's a new law.'

'Then I'm surprised they did not warn your mother.'

'They did,' she said. 'They wrote to me and said that Judith had been making enquiries and that she wanted to see me sometime in the future. They asked if I would agree to a meeting. I was reluctant because I couldn't go out without help to an agreed meeting place and I didn't want Judith to come here because I was afraid she might cause a disturbance.' She turned to me. 'I was wrong, of course, but I tried gently to discourage it. They wrote back and explained that you had a right to get in touch with me but that first you would be counselled and under the circumstances they would try to discourage you from coming here. In any case they didn't think you would follow it up, not for a while anyway. But, of course, they

107

never told me that you were coming in spite of what I said. They should have done that.'

'I didn't tell them,' I said. 'I was afraid that you might not agree. I came down here with the idea of trying to find you myself and then if there was no other way, I would have gone to the adoption society in Southampton for their help. Then I saw the advertisement. Although I couldn't be sure it was you, the name was the same and it was the only Carey in the area. Even then I wasn't certain. Everything seemed to fit, though.'

They both listened attentively. 'So that's how it happened,' said my mother. 'We've so much to talk about and you must have many questions you want answered. I'll do my best, but not tonight. I'm very tired now. I think we all need a good night's sleep and we'll talk tomorrow. Will you take me up, dear?'

I went across and helped her into her wheelchair and followed her from the room. At some point John must have gone unnoticed, for Mr Carey was alone. He had poured himself another drink and ignored my murmured goodnight.

Before I left her room, my mother kissed me and held me fast.

'I'm sorry,' I said, my voice breaking. 'I didn't want it to happen like this.'

'Something as important as this was not likely to disappear without affecting us all. It's the best way,' she said.

'That old photograph – was it me?'

'Yes. I think that was the point when we might have talked about it if the others hadn't been there. Don't you agree?'

'Perhaps. It's difficult to say now. Perhaps that wasn't the time and it had to be like this.'

Before I left the room, she stretched out her hand

and reached for her Bible. 'I pray for you every night, Judith. Whatever happens I want you to remember that.'

From my bedroom I heard my mother and Mr Carey talking long into the night, but he didn't sound angry. Daniel had been right, after all, and she had known all the time. He had been so sure about that. It was brave of her to speak up in front of us all but it was the way I would expect her to do it. I was beginning to understand this feeling of knowing the right thing to do, even when it was going to be difficult and you couldn't see where it would lead. Just like knowing that I had to leave here at the earliest opportunity and then perhaps the family could carry on as they used to. They could only do that if I was out of the way.

The next morning I found that John had gone off somewhere for the day and Mr Carey and Sophie had also left after an early breakfast. My mother and I were alone with no interruptions.

'The people I'm sorry for,' she said, 'are your parents. How much do they know?'

'They know I have found you but not that I was working here.'

'I feel in a way that I've taken you from them.'

'I think you've helped me to understand them better.'

'You will want to know about your father,' she said. 'He was killed in a car crash before we were married. I had no money of my own and when I left my job to have you they didn't want me back. My parents weren't prepared to help me either. They never liked Mike and at that time one didn't have so much help from the state. I didn't see much of a future for you with me and I made enquiries about adoption. They told me they knew of a nice couple who longed to have a baby. I really thought it was the best thing for you.'

'Is that the whole reason?'

'No, it isn't,' she said slowly. 'I was selfish. I hope I've changed now. I met Harry and fell in love with him. He was young, attractive and ambitious. He was also very persuasive, offering me security and love. At that time I had none of those things and they were irresistible. I couldn't turn them down. But there was one string attached. Harry knew about you. I never intended that he shouldn't, but he insisted that he was not going to take you on. He wanted a family, but he wanted his own and he didn't want someone else's child even if the father was dead. I accepted his terms and, when the adoption papers came through, I said goodbye to you, thinking that I would not have to face you or my conscience again. It never occurred to me that you might be unhappy and that you would blame me bitterly.'

'I don't any more,' I said, 'but I had to know. I think I can understand better now you've told me the reasons. Just the same I don't think I could have a baby of mine adopted.'

Her eyes were sad. 'I hope you'll never find yourself in that situation, Judith. Don't think it didn't hurt. It did. I never quite got over it though I think I would have done the same thing again under those circumstances. I was very much in love with Harry. You'll understand fully when you're in love yourself.'

'Does he mind very much?'

'Yes. It's come as a hard blow to him. He can't forgive me for not telling him before. I sympathize with him. He must see it, in a way, as a betrayal. But if he can bring himself to accept you, I believe it could compensate for the accident. It will take time but he might find he can do this for me. Can you understand?'

I nodded. 'I think so. But if you knew, why didn't you tell him?'

'Probably for the same reason that you kept quiet.

If he had found out he would probably have wanted you to leave and it was important that you should be given time to tell me yourself.'

'If you knew, why did you offer me the job?'

'Because I liked you and I was curious too. Perhaps it was to ease my conscience. You'd been so determined to find me and you wouldn't have come unless you wanted to find out about me and your past. I owed you that. What surprised me was that you asked me so few questions.'

'Because I was afraid you might realize who I was. I wanted more time and gradually I grew fond of you and wanted to help you and I was afraid of what telling you would do. It was more difficult as time went on.'

'So, apart from your parents and the family, no one else knows?'

'I told Daniel. At least, he almost guessed.'

'Daniel?' She looked puzzled. 'I didn't realize you were so friendly with him.'

I hesitated. 'We used to talk when I went over to see Mrs Bill. He kept asking questions so I thought I'd better tell him rather than let him guess. He was afraid in some way or other I was going to let you down. He won't tell anyone, of course.'

'I agree. Daniel is dependable and I'm fond of him. I shall tell Mrs Bill myself, of course. We can't tell one and keep it from the other.'

'He had rather a bad time himself, didn't he? With his father being killed and his mother dying when he was young.'

'Yes, but he had Mrs Bill. He thinks the world of her.'

We had finished breakfast and I followed her into the sitting room.

'Sit down, dear. You know you're welcome to stay here as long as you wish. I'd like you to, of course. The sooner the family gets used to having you around, the

111

better. The only thing is, I'm concerned about your parents. They will want you back some time. After all, they are your family.'

I hesitated. Then I said, 'I've already decided. I must go back. It will make it much easier for everyone and you've got someone coming to help you at the end of the week.'

I was glad that she didn't try to persuade me to stay. 'I shall miss you,' was all she said. Then, presently, 'You'll come back and see us sometime, won't you? You'll write too?'

I nodded. It was too early to make any promises. 'I feel I shall be able to manage better at home now. I think I've learned that from you. You're such a calm person. You understand how people feel and you don't upset them. I hope I'm better at that now.'

I sat beside her holding her hand. It was a tremendous relief not to have to pretend any more. 'Isn't it funny?' I said. 'Before I came here I thought that as soon as I saw you, I would know you were my mother. I thought there would be some special feeling between us, but it wasn't like that at all. I felt no particular bond. Now I love you and it seems so *right* that we belong to each other.'

'Not all mothers and daughters have this feeling,' she said. 'I think we're lucky, as though we've been given this gift to compensate for the lost years.'

'That's a lovely thought. Today I feel different — more complete. I've something to build on now.'

'Judith, I have something for you.' She reached for her bag in which she kept the things she needed throughout the day, her books and needlework and things like that. 'I ordered it some time ago and have been waiting for an opportunity to give it to you. This seems to me the right moment.'

She handed me a cardboard box. I opened it and took

112

out a black leather-bound Bible. It was beautiful to hold, with gold-edged leaves. I opened it and on the front page read in her neat handwriting, 'To Judith' and underneath she had written a text in quotes: 'Cast your cares on the Lord and he will sustain you. Psalm 15:22.' She had signed it, 'From your loving mother.'

I flicked over the thin pages, pausing now and then to read a passage. I'd never possessed a Bible before and it was a lovely thing to own, even if I never read it. The words seemed difficult to understand.

'Thank you,' I said. 'It's beautiful.'

She smiled. 'One day you must try reading it. It's not like an ordinary book. You'll find the words do speak to you.'

I put it back in its box. I felt it was much too nice to use. I might get marks on it and I wanted to keep it for ever to remind me of her.

'It's strong, you know,' she said. 'Made to last a lifetime. I hope it will become very worn.'

Chapter Fifteen

Early the next morning I said goodbye to my mother.
I tried not to show my real feelings because I knew it
would upset her. In many ways it was going to be worse
for her than it was for me. She was losing two people
she was used to, Mrs Bill and me, and she was going
to be entirely dependent on a stranger, though of course
she would soon get used to the experienced woman that
Mr Carey had arranged for her.

We made no arrangements to meet again. She would
certainly never be able to come and see me or even travel
part of the way for a meeting and it didn't seem at all
probable that I would ever come back. It was too far
and in any case I would not have the courage to face
the whole family again. The only thing that helped was
the conviction that I was doing the right thing. I had
to be gone before Mr Carey or Sophie came home again.
Perhaps then the family would be able to settle down
and forget about me.

Her last words to me were, 'Keep in touch, dear.
There's always the post.'

When it came to saying goodbye to Mrs Bill I hugged
her frail body, so different now from the plump cheerful
person who had so kindly helped me to settle down
when I first came. And because I suddenly knew that
I would never see her again, I whispered fiercely, 'See
you soon', and turned quickly away.

Daniel took me to the station and I sat beside him
struggling against tears. He couldn't stand that and I
wanted our last moments together to be happy. He

didn't say much either, which gave me time to get a grip on myself.

As we turned into the station, he said, 'I'm going to miss you, Judith. You'll come back again soon?'

'I don't know yet.'

'You haven't told me what happened.'

'I will now.' There was another twenty minutes before the train was due to leave and I told him everything that had happened in the last two days.

'So you don't have to go?'

'I must. I want to tell my parents about it and I'll find a job at home.'

'I'd try to stop you, but I believe you're right.'

I grinned at him. 'I'm glad you think so too. That makes it easier. Could you wait while I make a phone call?'

I walked back to the call box and dialled the number. Then I heard Mum's voice and pressed the button.

'Mum, it's Judith. I'm coming home.'

She had to want me. I wasn't prepared for anything else.

'Today? You're coming home today?' She was definitely pleased.

'I should be at home about six. I'll ring you from the station.'

'Your father will meet you. How long can you stay?'

'I'm leaving here. I'm coming home for a bit.'

'It will be good to see you, Judith. Even if only for a while.'

There was another thing I had to be sure of. 'What about Dad? How will he feel?'

'He'll be glad, love. You don't have to worry about that.'

My money had run out. I put down the receiver. Daniel had parked the car and was getting out my bags. He carried them over to the ticket office and waited while I bought my ticket. Then he came onto the platform with me, and humped the bags onto the train. We stood on the platform together.

'I want your address.' He put his hand in his pocket and brought out a pencil and paper. I gave it to him. There seemed nothing more to say.

'Well, you'd better get on,' he said gruffly.

'Thanks for everything, Daniel. You've been great.'

He stood there looking down at me. 'I could have been more than that,' he said. He bent and kissed me then, stirring up all sorts of feelings. The guard was coming along the platform closing doors. He released me and said, 'Goodbye, Judith. Take care.'

I stood in the corridor waving to him as the train pulled away and then went back to my seat. I slept most of the way home, feeling remote from reality.

Dad was waiting for me outside the station in the old car. 'I reckoned you'd be on this one,' he said. 'Your mother says you'll be staying a bit longer this time.'

'That's right, Dad.'

'Everything all right?' He glanced at me as he negotiated the traffic. 'Didn't lose your job or anything?'

I smiled. Better not say I had, or he'd think the worst of me. 'No, not really. It was temporary anyway. I'd had enough.'

'Wanted to come home, eh?'

'Yes. It was time. I'll look for something locally.'

'Thought it might turn out like that. Now you've satisfied your curiosity, you'll want to settle down at home again. I don't have to tell you that your mother and I are glad you've decided that way. We thought all along you'd made a mistake, but you had to find it out for yourself.'

'No, it wasn't a mistake, Dad. It was something I

116

wanted to do, but it's good to be home again.' I couldn't tell him how much I dreaded the future.

'Of course it is.' He was talking rather loudly, perhaps so that I could hear him over the noise of the traffic, but I remembered he always used to talk like that when he was unsure of himself. 'In a week or two you'll forget all that and you'll feel as though you never left home. I may as well say your mother and I are prepared to let bygones be bygones.'

I didn't want to start an argument, but I had to put it straight with him. 'You don't understand, Dad, I've changed. I'm not the same person who went away. I hope I'm nicer now.'

He glanced at me quickly. 'You don't have to explain,' he said, smiling now. 'We'll get on together all right.'

Mum gave me a lovely welcome when we reached home. I was ravenous and she had cooked a special meal.

Gradually we settled down to the old routine. For them I think it was simply a return to the old days, except that I was nicer and more considerate. For me it was very different. I felt the old irritations, things that I had forgotten used to annoy me, and it was worse because I was at home all the time except when I was out looking for a job. Most of my friends were working and, although I saw them sometimes in the evenings. I was on my own most of the time.

During those lonely days I often used to take out my new Bible from its box and read the words my mother had written – 'Cast your cares on the Lord and he will sustain you.' I found them comforting and as I turned the pages, I stopped here and there to read a passage. A lot of it I didn't understand, but every now and then I came across words that did speak to me and seemed to fit my mood exactly.

I took to reading it regularly and sometimes, in the privacy of my room, I knelt to pray. The prayer was nearly always the same and sometimes I found myself crying over it. 'Please help me, God. Surely my whole life isn't going to be like this. I can't bear it. Please tell me what to do.' And each time I felt oddly comforted, like that day in the forest when I was sure there was somebody beside me.

At last I got a job in the department store where I had worked before. Things began to improve and I made new friends. Each day I waited eagerly for the post. I longed for a letter from my mother and I couldn't understand why she didn't write, but nothing came. Nor did I have a letter from Daniel. Perhaps they were waiting to hear from me but I had nothing to say. I was afraid that if I wrote they would see how unhappy I was. Never a day went by that I did not long to be back. In spite of friends, city life was not for me and I missed the quiet of the forest, especially now the summer days were long and hot. I felt suffocated under the artificial lights of the store, serving people who never seemed to have heard of manners. When at the end of the day I stepped onto the streets in the rush hour, the noise and fumes of the traffic nauseated me. Maybe I shall get used to it, I thought.

Then, one evening when Dad had gone away for a few days on business, something happened that shattered me.

I wanted some drawing pins and Mum suggested that I might find some in the top drawer of Dad's desk. I would never have gone there normally and now I pulled open the drawer, revealing neat piles of letters and tins containing rubber bands, paper clips and so on. As I reached for the tin of drawing pins I dislodged some of the letters and it was then that I noticed one in my mother's handwriting and it was addressed to me.

I took it out and saw that it had been opened. I pulled it out of the envelope and read the date. It had been

118

written a month ago. I read on, hungry for news. My mother said she missed me but that the new Mrs Spencer was quite pleasant and helpful. Mrs Bill hadn't been at all well. Then she added bits of news about the rest of the family. Nothing spectacular, but why was it in Dad's desk and opened? For some reason he had deliberately kept it from me. Trembling with anger, I put the letter in my pocket and closed the drawer.

I didn't say anything to Mum, but inside I was boiling. How dare he interfere with my mail! What right had he, especially when he was always so self-righteous.

The next days were busy in the store, but it was at the back of my mind all the time. I would tackle him about the letter as soon as he returned and tell him exactly what I thought of him. Whatever his reason, I would never forgive him for this.

I couldn't even reply to the letter, feeling as I did. How could I tell my mother what had happened and why I had not replied before? Better not to write at all.

Restless and unhappy, I opened my Bible. Not that it would help me over this, but at least it might take my mind off it for a while and calm me down. I turned the pages, reading passages here and there. I found it difficult to concentrate on whole chapters at a time, but as I glanced down a column, suddenly a passage seemed to stand out. I went back over it. 'Be kind and compassionate to one another, forgiving each other, just as in Christ God forgave you.'

It brought me up short. Kind and compassionate? Forgiving? That was all right in reasonable circumstances, but not in mine. I couldn't be expected to forgive something like Dad had done to me. I certainly would not – could not – forgive that.

But that phrase kept returning to me. It would not leave my mind, however hard I tried to ignore it. I wished I had never set eyes on those words because, far from being able to forget it, it was made absolutely clear to me that not only was I to forgive the letter incident, but I must forgive something far deeper and longstanding. I was to forgive my mother for giving me for adoption and I must forgive my parents for concealing it from me.

I argued with God. I protested, made excuses, but in the end I said, 'All right, God. You win, but you've got to help me.'

Before Dad came home the next night, all the anger had drained out of me. I even felt sorry for him.

I waited until Mum had gone up to bed, then I took the letter out of my bag and handed it to him.

'I found this in your desk, Dad. It was addressed to me.'

He went quite white. He ignored the letter and went over to the window and stood with his back to me. 'May I ask what you were doing in my desk?' he demanded.

'I wanted some drawing pins and Mum suggested I should look there. As I took the tin out, I saw the letter.'

He turned round to face me. 'I was going to give it to you in due course. It came at a time when you were just beginning to settle down. I saw the postmark and I believed it was best that you should not be reminded of something that is over and done with. It was very wrong of your natural mother to try and take you from us and I did it for your own peace of mind.'

I was surprised that I felt no anger at his arrogance.

'She would never do that, Dad. In fact she thought I should come back home. But in any case, it was my letter and you had no right to hide it from me, nor was it yours to open and read.' I tried to speak gently. 'I've found it now and sometime I'll reply to it. But I want you to promise that you will never interfere with my mail again.'

'I'll make no promises.'

'Then I can't stay here. Dad, surely you can see this is wrong?' I pleaded with him. I understood how difficult it was for him to admit he was in the wrong. 'I believe you when you say you did it thinking it was for the best, but I'm not a child. Hiding her letters isn't going to stop me loving my mother, any more than receiving them won't stop me loving you and Mum. I love you all.'

His attitude changed then. His voice broke as he said, 'You're right, Judith. I'm sorry. Maybe I did the wrong thing but I give you my word it won't happen again. I just want to say I'm grateful to you for taking it like this.' He passed his hand over his face and said, 'I'm so tired, I think I'll turn in.'

He left the room and I heard his steps going slowly upstairs.

'Thank you, God,' I said softly. 'Thank you for making it easy and for replacing anger with love.'

Chapter Sixteen

After that Dad and I got along much better. The letter was never mentioned again but in a way the incident brought us closer together. I think Dad was making a real effort to understand me. This meant he had to throw off some of his preconceived ideas, which wasn't easy for him. For my part I tried to avoid arguments, even if I didn't always agree with him. The atmosphere at home became much more relaxed and Mum seemed happier, too.

I was still unsettled but each day as I read the Bible and took to praying more often, I felt that God was taking control of my life and that he did have a purpose for me. I just had to be patient and face each day as it came.

Sometimes I tried to explain to Annie how I felt, but she thought I had taken leave of my senses.

'What you need is a boyfriend, Judith. You seem so particular. I've introduced you to one or two really nice guys, and yet you don't go for them. Are you still moping for your mother or was there someone else down south?' Like Daniel, Annie had an uncanny knack of touching on the truth.

'No,' I said, looking away from her. 'Give me a chance. I can't date a guy unless I'm really interested in him. I can't pretend.'

She looked at me closely. 'If you don't make up your mind soon, it'll be too late. The fellows like you, they really do. Why don't you give them a break?'

I suppose I had changed. I liked Annie's friends and enjoyed being with them, but I didn't want to get involved with anyone at the moment. The thought of Daniel was still too vivid and no one else measured up to him. Maybe I was destined to spend the rest of my life living on memories, I thought.

Then, something happened. I had finished work and, as usual, taken the bus home. As I turned into our street, I saw a familiar red van outside our house. I let myself in and then I heard his voice talking to Mum in the sitting room.

'Hullo,' I said.

'A friend of yours to see you,' said Mum. Daniel got up and kissed my cheek. 'Had to come this way,' he said. 'Couldn't pass without dropping in.'

We went out that evening, out of the town and into the beautiful countryside that surrounds Derby.

'What are you doing up here?' I asked.

'I just felt it was time I saw you,' he said. Sitting there beside him in the old van, still smelling of horses and oil even though he had cleaned it up, was bliss. Seeing that dear face and the familiar grin just filled all my needs.

'How is everyone?' I asked.

'Wondering what's happened to you. Why didn't you write?'

'I didn't have much to say. Please tell me everything. How's my mother?'

'All right. We miss you.' Then his face saddened. 'I'd better tell you first, Gran died.'

'Oh Daniel, how awful. I'm sorry.'

He didn't say anything for a moment and I knew he was struggling to control himself.

'We expected it. The doctor warned us. Just the same, it came as a shock. I miss her so much.'

'You must do. She was a lovely person.'

123

'It's one of the reasons I wanted to come and see you. To tell you and talk about her. She was very fond of you.'

'I know. And I was fond of her, too. I can hardly believe it. When did it happen?'

'Two weeks ago. She was in hospital. She was taken poorly again soon after you left. Just after the new housekeeper came. Just as well, perhaps.' He gave a wry grin. 'She didn't take to her very much. Not what she was used to, she said.'

'I can understand that. She used to run the place really, didn't she? My mother must miss her.'

'Yes. It's all changed now. What with you gone and Mrs Spencer there.'

'You'll get used to it, Daniel. How do you manage alone in the cottage?'

We were motoring along above the river. The country looked incredibly beautiful but the evening was saddened.

'Oh, I can manage all right. I can cook and look after myself, but it's so empty without her.'

We were approaching a village and Daniel drove into the car park of an old inn. 'Let's sit by the river and have a meal here,' he suggested.

We wandered down to the river hand in hand.

'What about you?' he asked. 'You seem different. Happier somehow. Are you?'

I thought about it. 'Yes, perhaps. But happy is not really the word. It's just that I don't worry about things any more.'

He looked at me thoughtfully. 'You've grown more like your mother, you know.'

I knew what he meant and it was true. 'I think I have, Daniel. I hope so, anyway.'

'Glad to be back in a town again, I expect. You've got friends here and you must have found it lonely sometimes in the forest.'

I shook my head. 'No. I miss it. I don't like the noise and crowds and I don't really like working in a department store all day. But then, I'm lucky to have a job.'

We had rounded a bend in the river and here there were trees and no one in sight. Daniel stopped and turned me to face him. 'Judith, it wasn't only to tell you about Gran that I came.'

'It doesn't matter why you came. It's just so good to see you.'

'I want to ask you to marry me.'

I lifted my eyes to meet his and I saw love in them. I touched his face and he bent his head and kissed me, a long passionate kiss.

'You've got to say yes after that,' he said. 'I know now that you feel the same way.'

'Oh yes, I do. I've loved you for such a long time. But I hadn't thought of marriage.'

'All girls think of it.' He grinned at me.

'What I mean is, I didn't think that you had marriage in mind. I've only just got home. Of course I want to marry you, but there are so many difficulties.'

'None that can't be overcome, given time. I won't rush you. All I want is your word. Your mother, of course, will be glad to have you near. You won't be living in the big house, so Mr Carey can't object. You could help out there sometimes, but only if you wanted to.'

I smiled. 'You've thought it all out, haven't you? It's Mum and Dad that are worrying me. They've just got used to having me around again.'

'Give them time to get used to the idea. I'm sure your mum will understand. She'll be happy for you if she knows it's what you want. When we're married you can come and visit them and have them down there. Judith, please say yes.'

He took me in his arms again and I had no power to resist. Just as I knew before it was the right time to come home, now it was time to begin a new kind of life with the man I loved.